I0621574

THE SOMETIME BRIDE

By
Ginny Baird

Published by
Winter Wedding Press

Copyright 2012
Ginny Baird
Trade Paperback
ISBN 978-0-9858225-0-7

Edited by Linda Ingmanson
Cover by Darleen Dixon

****

About the Author

From the time that she could talk, romance author Ginny Baird was making up stories, much to the delight -- and consternation -- of her family and friends. By grade school, she'd turned that inclination into a talent, whereby her teacher allowed her to write and produce plays, rather than write boring book reports. Ginny continued writing throughout college, where she contributed articles to her literary campus weekly, then later pursued a career managing international projects with the US State Department.

Ginny's held an assortment of jobs, including school teacher, freelance fashion model, and greeting card writer, and has published more than ten works of fiction and optioned nine screenplays. She's additionally published short stories, nonfiction and poetry, and admits to being a true romantic at heart.

Ginny is the author of bestselling novels *The Sometime Bride* and *Real Romance*, and has just launched her "Girls on the Go" series, which premiered with *Santa Fe Fortune*. She's a member of Romance Writers of America (RWA), the RWA Published Authors Network (PAN), and the RWA Published Authors Special Interest Chapter (PASIC).

Ginny lives with her family in Tidewater, Virginia. When she's not writing, Ginny enjoys cooking, biking and just about any word game, including crossword puzzles and Scrabble. She loves hearing from her readers by email at GinnyBairdRomance@gmail.com and can also be found on Facebook http://www.facebook.com/GinnyBairdRomance and Twitter @GinnyBaird.

****

Chapter One

Carrie St. John strode to the edge of the pool and tugged the ring from her finger. One year, six months, and four days exactly. *Yank.* The dang thing was stuck.

Carrie looked down in frustration at the glittering diamond offset by tiny emeralds. Beautiful, yes. But— *yank*, the ring worked free of her knuckle and glided off her narrow upper finger—only a poor reminder of a relationship gone sour.

Carrie clutched her hand around the meager gems, wondering if Wilson had paid more for them, he'd have been more reluctant to leave. Hogwash, she thought, tossing back her arm and prepping for a long throw. Wilson would have left regardless. And if it hadn't been for Teresa, it would have been for someone else.

But of all the rotten things to do! Take Carrie to a scenic country inn, then drop the bomb. More like a blazing comet, Carrie thought, feeling the raw burn in her heart as she lobbed the ring forward over the water. The engagement ring pitched in a perfect arch toward the water, then plopped beneath the surface with a deafening calm.

Mike Davis ran a flat palm along the bumpy bottom surface of the pool. It had to be down here somewhere, darn it! Four months of hard-earned commission down the chlorinated drain!

If Mike had had any inkling how callous Alexia could be, he would have never gone to the trouble. Not to mention the biting expense. Now if he couldn't find the darned ring, he'd be set back financially for nothing!

Already was set back financially for nothing, Mike reminded himself, feeling his lungs drain of air. This was his third dive under and still nothing doing.

Hey, wait a minute…

Mike fishtailed over to the center of the pool where something glistened against its bottom. Yep, that was it! Had to be…

Mike swept toward the gemstone like an alligator on the prowl, then plucked the tiny ring off the pool bottom, examining it through the blurry haze caused by pool lights and chemicals. No way. But it was. Somebody else's ring entirely. The ring Mike had presented to Alexia had been a solitaire.

Despite years of high school swim-team accomplishments, Mike felt his wind quickly abating. He'd been down here too long, he realized, angling toward the surface and pressing his heels off the bottom.

Mike rocketed skyward, another woman's engagement ring clutched in his hand. Another woman who was likely just as heartless as his Alexia. When Adam gave his rib to Eve, Mike thought, breaking into the chill of the evening, the poor schmuck hadn't realized the woman had plans to barbeque it!

Carrie let out a shriek as water barreled forth and a man emerged from the center of the pool.

He shook out his honey-blond head, then paddled over to the side where Carrie stood.

"Lose something?" he asked as Carrie backed up a step.

Carrie raised a hand to her cheek and stroked back hot tears. "Where on earth did you come from?" she demanded of this Poseidon-like god, whose eyes, she noticed, were as green as the Caribbean Sea. Though she didn't know why she'd noticed, or—more importantly—why she particularly cared.

"I came from the bottom of the pool," he said, his tone not the least bit friendly. "Where I ran into a little something that might just be yours."

With that, he pulled his right hand out of the water and gingerly steadied Carrie's engagement ring between his thumb and forefinger.

Despite his hostile tone, Carrie grudgingly admitted that this swim god was actually quite attractive. Alarmingly attractive, in a way that would make most women swoon. But not Carrie, she told herself, backing up another step. Attractive meant trouble, and, in the last four hours, Carrie St. John had endured enough trouble to last a lifetime.

"I'm sorry," she said, shaking her head, "you've got the wrong girl."

Well, that was one way to look at it, Mike thought, shifting his gaze between the ring pinched in his fingers and the enigmatic woman on the pool deck.

She was dressed in a summer sundress, wavy brown hair flowing to her shoulders. Her eyes, he thought, were just as dark. Although from this angle it was pretty hard to tell.

Mike braced himself on his arms as he rose from the water.

"Don't think so," he told her, lightly shaking off and extending his hand, palm up, in her direction.

"Excuse me?" she asked, trying her best to look indignant. There was a little pout to her mouth that looked almost appealing. Almost, Mike reminded himself, not quite. Brunettes, in general, meant trouble. And Alexia had taught him that trouble not only hurt like the dickens, it was darned expensive too.

"Your ring," Mike said, stepping forward.

"You have a lot of nerve…" she said, setting her chin. Yep, Mike told himself, they were definitely brown. Chocolate-brown eyes that could probably look enticingly warm were they not so heated with vehemence. "…intruding on my private moment!"

Mike laughed. "Intruding? But I was here first!"

She shuffled sandaled feet beneath the low hemline of her dress. Feet that were attached, Mike couldn't help but notice, to two very well-formed feminine ankles. "Well, if you were, I certainly didn't see…"

Mike arched his eyebrows, and she stopped. By the way her appreciative eyes had traveled from his damp pecs to his navel, sure as heck looked to Mike like she'd been seeing something.

"What I meant to say was—"

Mike walked forward and lifted a balled-up fist from the woman's side. "Here," he said, prying her fingers loose as she looked on with incredulity.

Mike pressed the ring into her palm. "Someone spent hard-earned money for that. Don't think it's very good of you to go throwing it away."

Carrie glared at the insolent man, wondering how he'd known exactly what she'd been doing. More puzzled still at how he dared intrude on her life. "Don't think it's very good of you to go telling a complete stranger how to run her affairs!"

"Oh, so it was only an affair, was it?" he asked, with a cool sheen to his evergreen eyes. Eyes that Carrie was quite certain could look enticing under different circumstances. "Somehow I imagined it was a heck of a lot more serious than that."

"Well, maybe," she said, flipping over his wrist and cramming the ring back into his hand. "You ought to think of something better to do with your overactive imagination than torment women you don't even know."

Carrie turned her back on him and started toward the inn. Of all the indignities. To be trounced upon by one man during dinner, then have a hunky dish like this one serve up insults for dessert.

"Hang on!" he called, hurrying to catch up with her. "Your ring!"

"Finders, keepers," she said, picking up her pace. But what Carrie most desperately didn't want to find herself doing was falling for another man. Especially one who looked like that in a pair of swim trunks—all six foot something of virile man, dripping wet... Criminy! Carrie scurried up the cold stone steps to the main building's front door. The flame was barely extinguished on her relationship with Wilson and here she was already playing with matches!

Carrie struggled against the notion of turning back toward her predator but knew he stood silently watching her at the bottom of those stairs. Silently—rugged, handsome, yes, darn it, handsome. And wet. Carrie's throat went dry at that last thought.

"What?" she asked, spinning abruptly on her heels. "What in the world are you staring at?"

But Mike, who truthfully didn't know, just stood there dumbfounded with this beautiful stranger's ring in his hand. Beautiful, indeed. There was a fine sweep of color that just dusted her cheekbones, and somehow—given all the crying she'd apparently been doing—Mike didn't imagine it was the magic of makeup. No, there was something much more powerful going on here. Something that made absolutely zero sense. And, for a lunatic instant, Mike found himself wishing he hadn't wasted his heartfelt offering on Alexia but had given it to this goddess instead.

Lunatic was right. Mike gazed up at the powdery quarter moon threading stardust through the trees, deciding he'd been out in the night air too long.

But whether he was crazy or not, Mike knew one thing and one thing only. Before she disappeared into the inn, and perhaps for eternity, he had to get her name.

"I was just wondering," he began tentatively, feeling the heat expand from his temples to the tops of his ears. "What your name is." Holy Christ. He was insane! Alexia's ring was still at the bottom of the pool, and here he was…what? Making eyes at another woman who'd just now broken some Romeo's heart?

"Why?" she asked, holding court at the top of the stairs but not looking half as menacing as she apparently intended.

"Just in case the law comes after me for stealing your ring," Mike raced in, thinking quickly. He gave her his best smile but found it impossible to tell whether she was charmed by it or not.

"Very funny."

He guessed not. "Seriously, I—"

"Name's Carrie, if you must know. Carrie St. John, and you can rest assured, uh…"

"Mike," he filled in with a grin.

"Mike," she said, clearing her throat and averting her eyes from his naked upper torso, which he'd noticed her perusing just the same. "You can rest assured I won't be calling the police on you anytime soon."

"Ah, so you do admit the ring was yours, after all."

Her eyes flashed as she turned and headed through the door.

Conniving male! They were all the same, every last one of them. And what, pray tell, did this dripping hunk of flesh plan to do with that information? Blackmail her? As if the entire world wouldn't find out soon enough. With Carrie's luck, it would make the morning edition.

Carrie let herself into her room and fell in a heap of emotion onto the bed. Her life couldn't possibly get any worse! First, Wilson brought her all the way here, to this gorgeous historic home—to tell her he's fallen in love with another woman. Then he left her, more like deserted her, in this love nest built for two, and had the gall to tell her to enjoy the rest of the weekend. His treat.

Carrie pressed her palms to her forehead to ward off her ensuing headache. But knew that it would come regardless. This was stress with a capital "S"! She'd been such a fool, had already invited six women to be her bridesmaids! And now she'd have to call each one and confess her misfortune.

And what was worse, what would truly be the worst part of all would be in facing her matchmaking grandmother. The grandmother Carrie had finally managed to convince she'd found a dashing bachelor to make "an honest woman" of her.

Carrie rolled over on the bed and clutched her pillow to her streaming cheeks. One time. Okay. But this was the second disaster she'd endured at the near-altar. What was it about her, Carrie wondered, that made men want to cut and run? Or worse still, rush straight into another woman's arms? Carrie had actually seen Teresa, knew exactly who the woman was. And though as a fellow stockbroker of Wilson's she certainly shared Wilson's business savvy, Carrie truthfully didn't find Teresa that much to look at.

And that made matters all the worse, Carrie admitted to herself, as her throat swelled tight and tears blazed trails down her cheeks. She couldn't blame Wilson's leaving her on something as base as hormones, or his sheer physical attraction to another woman. No, what had caused Wilson to leave ran deeper than that. When he'd looked beneath the surface of his relationship with both Teresa and Carrie, Teresa had won hands down.

Mike took another dive below the surface and cursed himself once again for his inability to find Alexia's ring. If she wasn't going to use it, she could have at least had the good grace to return it, not toss it in the pool.

What was it with all the women in this place? Had they made a silent pact to simultaneously ditch their men in this affronting fashion? Maybe that was what this vacation locale was all about. Some sort of fantasy dumping ground for all disenchanted females. Bring your man to the Sawyers House and be rid of him for good! Elegant starlight pool, suitable for ring-tossing!

Mike was just about to call it a night when he saw something shimmer at the far corner of the pool bottom. Aha! It was his ring all right. One perfect solitaire that obviously hadn't been enough to do the job. *"Marry you?"* Alexia had scoffed. *"You can't be serious?"* Only as serious as a heart attack, a heart attack Mike had sorely wished he'd had rather than face the blistering look in Alexia's cool blue eyes. *"But, sweetheart,"* she'd told him, *"everything's been so good so far. Why would you want to go and ruin it now?"*

Gee, call him a fool, but somehow Mike hadn't seen wanting to spend the rest of his life with someone as "ruining" things. What an idiot he'd been, believing that someone like Alexia could possibly care. Even in refusing his ring, she'd been the quintessential ice woman. Couldn't she even have pretended to have been impressed by the half-carat diamond?

Instead, when their server had arrived with dessert, she'd pushed the small velvet box aside and urged Mike to be "mature" about things. She certainly wasn't ready for that kind of commitment—and he could keep the ring.

Mike had shoved the box back in front of her, saying she could hang on to it until she felt ready. She'd given him a thin smile and said, *"Fine."* It was only because he'd followed her when she'd excused herself to the ladies' room that he'd witnessed her break the delicate ring free from its velvet prison and lob it into the pool before climbing into her black Jaguar and driving out of his life.

Just like that.

Alexia hadn't even planned to say good-bye.

Mike sat on the end of a lounge chair and studied the two rings in his hand. One glistening solitaire, the other an elegant arrangement of emeralds and diamonds. For all Mike knew, he thought, casting a tired gaze over the pool surface, there were others like these down there. Dozens, maybe. Heck, if he looked long enough, he might even find thousands.

He could start his own business: Ring Finders Unlimited. He'd make a fortune on broken hearts...

Mike blinked back the heat in his eyes and stared up at the star-speckled night, realizing just how cynical he'd become.

It was really too late to drive back to the city, and his room for the night was bought and paid for. Plus, he still had mystery woman's ring in the palm of his hand. Mike didn't know how, but some way before he left here tomorrow, he was going to get that woman to take back her ring. Then maybe she could return it properly to whoever had given it to her in the first place.

Not that it was Mike's normal style to go inserting himself in other people's relationships, but someone had to wise the female species up to the damage it was doing out there. And, since he had nothing left to lose, Mike thought, tightening his grip around his solitaire, it might as well be him.

****

Chapter Two

Carrie sat at the small breakfast table, absentmindedly stirring her coffee.

"Good morning," a deep baritone echoed from above her.

Carrie looked up at the dapper man in chinos and a button-down shirt. "Mike! I almost didn't recognize you with your clothes on!"

A couple at the next table set down their grapefruit spoons and stared.

"I mean," Carrie backpedaled, perspiration sweeping her hairline, "dry." Oh, Criminy. Carrie picked up her cup, but Mike just grinned and pulled out a chair.

"Mind if I join you?" he asked.

Now that was a loaded question for eight o'clock in the morning. Carrie picked up the Style Section of the newspaper and rapidly fanned her face. "Sure, why not?" Anything, she thought. Anything to get this Greek Adonis to sit—and her to stop babbling like an idiot in this public place.

"Listen," he said, squaring his chair in with the table. "I think we got off on the wrong foot last night."

"Look, Mike," Carrie said, reaching a hand across the table to touch his arm, then instantly regretting it. It had to be over eighty degrees inside, with the air-conditioning in this antiquated building malfunctioning, and yet, still, the contact sent shivers up her spine. "As far as I'm concerned, the two of us aren't even going anywhere. So, wrong foot or no, it's all water under the bridge."

"Or, into the pool," he said with a smile that pinned her in place even though a very big part of her longed to spring from her chair and race from the room. What was it with her? What in the world was she afraid of? Mike...? And if it was terror she felt, then why did every inch of her skin vibrate with electric fire each time his sea-green eyes settled on hers?

Carrie took a very long, deliberate sip of water, then set down her glass. "You know, I never got your last name," she said with a smile she hoped looked pleasantly interested, not recklessly giddy.

"Davis," he said as a server sauntered over. "No," he told her as she tilted the silver coffee carafe, "I'm not staying."

"You're not?" Carrie asked before she could stop herself.

Mike arched one eyebrow, and the slightest tingle took hold of Carrie's tailbone. Damn it, she thought, shaking off the confusion. She was not attracted to this man, not attracted one iota. And she was going to prove it. To him— and the rest of the world, as well.

"Please," Carrie said in her most gracious Southern tone. "Do stay. It's the least I can do for..."

Their waitress colored slightly as Carrie's words fell off.

Mike accepted a cup of coffee then met Carrie's eyes with a sly smile. "You know," he whispered as their server departer. "I think you almost embarrassed that woman."

"Truth be told," Carrie admitted, taking a sip of coffee that had grown lukewarm, "I almost embarrassed myself."

Mike tore open a sugar packet and dumped the contents into his cup. "Do tell."

But Carrie didn't want to tell—tell this man any more than she had to. For, in a very big way, she already feared she'd told him way too much. Maybe not in so many words but certainly with her eyes. Guy who looked like that was bound to be experienced. Would certainly know when a woman was…what? Ogling him? Impossible. Carrie St. John was a business professional, a seasoned woman of the world. She did not ogle. She appraised. And every one of Mike's assets, darn it, were starting to add up.

"I never kiss and tell," Carrie said, realizing afterwards just how flirtatious that sounded.

Carrie flagged down the waitress and asked for another glass of water, wondering if she wouldn't be better off having the waitress dump the whole pitcher in her lap.

Mike stirred his coffee, then set aside the spoon. "Okay by me," he assured her with earnest green eyes. "Believe me, I won't be pressing you for details."

Carrie shifted in her chair, wondering why his gentlemanly assertion made her heart drop down to her belly. It wasn't that she wanted him pressing her—for details.

Criminy! She was a mess!

Carrie gratefully grabbed her refilled water and downed half the glass in one long swallow. "Won't be here for too much longer anyhow," she said, searching for a reasonable-sounding way out of the corner she'd painted herself into. "Least ways, not long enough to engage in long-winded conversation."

"I see," Mike said, studying her white-knuckled grip on her water glass. "So, then, where will you be going back to?"

"Mill Creek," she told him, feeling the room lightly spin around her. As ridiculous as it seemed, there was something about him that made her want to forget about going home altogether. Maybe it was in the heart-stopping way he looked at her, even when he pretended to be making normal conversation. Or maybe it was in the way he looked when he was half undressed…

Carrie bit into her bottom lip as Mike fell back in his chair with surprise.

"No kidding? I'm right next door in Redfields!"

"So what are you doing up here?" she asked, trying to keep her thoughts on the straight and narrow. Straight and narrow? Holy cow! Totally wrong image! What on earth was wrong with her? Never in her life had her mind been so carnally occupied!

His eyes fell to his coffee cup. "Maybe it's best if I don't kiss and tell either."

"You mean," Carrie asked with surprise, "you were here with a woman?"

He looked up, little wrinkles creasing his brow. "You find that so amazing?"

Actually, what Carrie found amazing was that any woman in her right mind who'd come here with Mike in the first place wouldn't still be here with him now. "What happened?" Carrie asked, softening her voice in concern. "I mean, certainly you don't have to tell me, but—"

"She dumped me," Mike said, bright eyes darkening. "Sayonara. Just like that. Didn't even have the courtesy to say good-bye. Simply walked out at dinner and never came back."

"No…" Carrie said, catching her breath on the unbelievable. That actually sounded worse than what had happened to her!

"Wish I could say it wasn't so," Mike said with a shake of his head, "particularly after all the… Well, never mind," he told her, fingering the rings through his pants pocket. "None of that matters much now."

Mike reached into his chinos and pulled out the pair of rings. "Not quite a matching set," he said, laying them on the table. But quite an attractive pair just the same."

Carrie blanched and looked up. "Are you telling me that... Now, wait a minute—"

Mike nodded. "Uncanny as it seems, my ring got tossed in the pool as well. Maybe it's some sort of unwritten bylaw to staying in this place."

"Only when the guys involved are first-class jerks," Carrie said with a hard edge to her voice.

A rosy band of color swept across the bridge of her nose. "Oh, sorry... Didn't mean it to—"

"So, you're assuming it was somehow my fault?" Mike asked.

"Well, it's only natural. If she felt strongly enough to throw your ring in—"

And here he'd actually been feeling sorry for her. Had been entertaining these ridiculous thoughts. Ideas that he and this fellow lovelorn soul might actually have something in common. Or maybe he'd just been deluding himself to keep his mind off his raging heartache.

Mike pushed back abruptly from the table. "Enjoy the rest of your stay," he said, dabbing his mouth with his napkin.

"Wait!" Carrie said, leaning forward across the table and attempting to grab his arm. But it was too late. He'd already laid a ten dollar bill on the table and walked away.

Carrie tipped the waitress, then hurriedly made her way out the front door. Bright sunlight spun gold through lilac bushes lining the cobblestone walk in front of her. Overhead, morning birds called out in song as the fragrance of early summer laced the air.

This was absurd! Carrie didn't even know where in the inn he'd been staying, much less what kind of car he drove. For all she knew, he'd already gone!

Carrie looked down in a cold sweat at the two rings nestled in her damp palm. She hadn't even wanted one, and now she'd been saddled with two of them! One from a man she thought she'd known but actually didn't know at all. The other from a virtual stranger!

Carrie raced down the path, then halted where it met the gravel drive. Off to the left and down at the bottom of the grassy hill, lay the gazebo—and the swimming area.

Of course, she thought, squaring her shoulders and taking off in that direction.

Mike sat at the end of the chaise lounge, knowing it was more than just Alexia. His failings at romance had an awful lot to do with himself. Hadn't he just proven that back at the inn ten minutes ago? Fifteen minutes with a woman who didn't know him from Adam and she'd already pitched him straight into that flaming barbeque pit.

Well, fine, maybe monogamy wasn't all it was cracked up to be anyway. Just because he'd always thought he'd wanted a wife and family didn't necessarily mean that was in his cards. And every good poker player knew when to hold 'em and when to fold 'em. Maybe, at thirty-eight, it was time Mike cashed in his chips. He'd always yearned to do something different. Move to the Caymans, maybe, and open up that dive shop he'd always dreamed about.

Before, with gold-digging Alexia, he'd been reluctant to leave his "stable" job in real estate and pursue something more daring. Now, he had nothing in the world to stop him.

"Thought I'd find you down here."

Mike looked up in surprise to find Carrie standing radiant in the sunlight.

"I believe I have something of yours," she said, walking toward him and turning over his solitaire in her hand.

Mike stood. "That was awfully nice of you. But you didn't have to. Particularly after the way I—"

She gave him the soft smile he'd always known her capable of. "Didn't mean to offend you—or imply that you, personally, were any kind of jerk. That's just...uh, been my own unfortunate experience."

"Yeah, well, unfortunately, my experience with women hasn't run much better."

A cool morning breeze lifted off the water and fanned Carrie's long skirt around her legs. "We're a real pair, aren't we?" she asked, bending down to smooth out the clingy material that Mike kind of wished she'd left in place. It had been doing a spectacular job at emphasizing the curves of her luscious legs.

"A couple of losers, you mean?" he asked, wrinkling his brow. "Now, I don't think I'd go as far to say that."

"Losers, absolutely not," Carrie said, coming over and sitting in a nearby chair. "Just down on our luck a bit at the moment."

"I'll say," Mike said, pulling up another chair and sitting beside her. "Worked a good long time to buy that ring. That last house, especially, was a bear to sell. But I knew if I didn't have the commission—"

"You're in real estate?" she asked, looking amused.

"What's so surprising about that?"

"Oh nothing, really," she said, pursing her lips and looking toward the pool. "Just somehow I envisioned you in a line of work a little more—physical."

Mike spurted a laugh. "Lifeguard, you mean?" He pondered the notion of giving her mouth-to-mouth as she turned her very kissable lips toward his. Lips that had no business looking so damn inviting on such a downright disastrous morning.

Carrie shrugged two silky white shoulders that peeked out from beneath her halter-style dress. "Well, sure. That—or a rock climber. Firefighter. Policeman…"

Carrie bit her tongue, realizing how very much she sounded as if she were exercising her fantasies. And if she put her mind to it, Carrie was quite certain she could come up with one or two of those involving the well-built man beside her—clothed or not.

It was probably getting close to checkout and time for Carrie to get back to her room. Her first order of business was calling her grandmother to tell her tomorrow afternoon's bridal shower was off. It would be a sorrowful disappointment to her grandmother and all of her grandmother's old friends who'd worked so hard in the planning. Not only that, they'd all been expecting to meet the groom! And here Carrie was having to show up empty-handed.

Carrie cast a sideways glance at the man beside her, a totally absurd notion popping into her brain. No, he wouldn't. She wouldn't even dare to ask!

"You know the worst part about all of this?" Mike asked, still studying the water. But Carrie truly couldn't imagine anything worse than the look on her grandmother's face when Carrie confessed she'd let another eligible bachelor slip right through her ineffectual fingers. "It's my reunion."

"Reunion?" Carrie asked.

Mike grimaced. "High school. And for once, I thought I'd finally have a fighting chance to prove them wrong."

Carrie heaved a deep sigh, grateful that her own twentieth was still a good, safe five years away. Other than business success, she'd had nothing to show for herself at her tenth, so hadn't gone. By her twentieth, she'd been certain she'd have a dashing man—perhaps even a baby or two—on her arm. Now, she wasn't so certain.

"Which one is it?" Carrie asked, thinking she knew but feeling it only polite to ask.

"Twentieth," Mike reported with a frown. A frown that didn't much become him, Carrie decided. His was an open, expressive face meant for love and laughter. Carrie blinked hard at the thought, wondering where that love part had come from. "And the sad thing is—after all these years— I'm only going to prove those fellows right."

"Which fellows?" Carrie asked.

"The ones who voted me 'Most Likely to Remain a Bachelor'."

"Hmm."

Mike turned to look at her, his eyes catching a glint of sunshine bouncing off the spreading oaks that surrounded the pool area. They were deep-green eyes and swimming like the ocean, a deep, lulling current Carrie was quite sure she could get lost in if she wasn't very, very careful. "That's not why I proposed to Alexia, if that's what you're thinking."

"Alexia?" Carrie pondered. "Sounds very— sophisticated."

"That's a polite way to put it."

Carrie laughed. "Well, I'm sure not the most objective one to pass judgment at the moment."

"And you and yours?" Mike asked. "Mr. So-Wonderfully-Terrific you felt compelled to chuck his ring into the pool?"

"Well, I doubt I could be very objective about him either," Carrie admitted, sheepishly studying her toes through the straps of her sandals. "But then again, men like Wilson Haywood don't deserve much objectivity."

Mike cracked a grin. "Wilson, huh? Sounds very—sophisticated.

Carrie's lips pulled into a smile.

"Say," Mike began, his eyes lighting with mischief. "I've got it! How about we get your Wilson together with my—"

"Afraid it wouldn't work," Carrie said, shaking her head. "Wilson's already taken."

"That fast? That's gotta be some kind of... Oh," Mike said, his smile fading in understanding. "No wonder you chucked his ring! So tell me, what was it with this guy? Deaf, blind, or stupid? Or possibly all three?"

Carrie let loose a belly laugh, delighted with the turn this conversation had taken. "All three, I guess," she said, giggling into her hand. "And your girl? Alexis?"

"Alexia," Mike corrected.

Carrie shrugged.

"You're right," Mike agreed. "Really doesn't matter anymore now, does it? I mean, you give a gal the perfect ring..."

Carrie suddenly realized she still had Mike's ring clutched in her hand with the other. "Oh my goodness," she said, attempting to pass it over. "Here! I almost forgot!"

Mike shook his head. "Finders, keepers."

"Now, wait a minute! You left this on the table by accident!"

Mike gave her a sly wink. A wink that did terrific things for the tingles that had been lying dormant in her spine. "You quite sure of that?"

"Of course, I'm sure. You went to all the trouble to dig it out of the pool, didn't you? The ring obviously still means something to you, even if the woman you intended to wear it doesn't."

Yeah, Mike thought, that ring still meant a lot. Like about three thousand dollars, an amount he honestly couldn't afford to throw away, not with his renewed plans to move to the Caymans. If he was to make that long-lost dream a reality, he'd have to start counting every dime.

Mike stretched a reluctant hand in Carrie's direction and took back the ring.

"Quite a game of ring toss we're playing here, eh, Mike?" Carrie asked with the most compelling smile he'd seen on her face yet. Boy, wouldn't his old high school buddies just die if Mike showed up with someone like that on his arm. Classy but genuine, with an unguarded warmth that seemed to be getting hotter by the minute.

Mike wiped an arm across his moistened brow. "Got that right," he said, giving her a smile. "And it's getting a little warm out for ring toss…" Her dark eyes widened, expecting who knew what kind of proposition. "But perfect for a swim," he finished as he watched the color rush back into her face.

Yessiree, she was quite a looker. Would knock every one of that high school gang out cold! If only Mike could think up a way to take her.

"Oh no," Carrie said, scrambling to her feet. "I'm not much for swimming."

"No?" Mike asked, standing beside her. "But why in heaven's name not? It's hot as blazes out—"

Yes, damn it, Carrie could quite appropriately feel the heat. It was sticking to every inch of her with gummy fingers that prickled her skin with perspiration and sent a cascade of droplets sliding down her cleavage. But no way in Hades was she going to let a man as perfectly formed as Mike Davis see her practically naked in a swimsuit—even her modest, one-piece kind. Carrie wore her dresses ankle-length for a reason, a reason that centered mostly around her buttocks and thighs.

"Besides," Carrie added hastily, "I've got some packing to do."

"Packing?" Mike asked, looking crestfallen. "But I thought for sure you were staying. Isn't there some sort of two-night weekend minimum at this place?"

"Why yes, but—"

"Well, then, what's your hurry?"

And why, Carrie wondered, scrunching up her lips, was he trying so hard to convince her to stay? "I've got things to do," she informed him. "Arrangements to— cancel."

"And tomorrow will be too late?"

"Might be," she told him, meaning it absolutely. Too late for a lot of things. Particularly her heart. This man, Mike Davis, had an unsettling effect on her. His whole wounded-puppy-dog ploy had worked wonders at disarming her emotion. Emotion she'd sworn only last night, as she stood weeping by this same pool, she would indefinitely keep under wraps.

"Aw, come on," he coaxed with a crooked grin. "I'll bet your room's already paid for."

She looked at him and blinked. The fact was, Wilson had already footed the bill.

"Hey, I'm not proposing anything indecent here." For some reason, that admission did not make Carrie happy. "Only a little attempt at sweet revenge."

Carrie eyed him suspiciously. "Revenge how?"

"Revenge in our not letting them ruin our weekend."

Big, fat chance of that one, Carrie thought. More than her weekend had been ruined. How about her life? "Listen, Mike, it's a sweet idea, your wanting to keep me company and all…"

Now that was putting it mildly, Mike thought, feeling the rising sun beat down through his stuffy cotton shirt. Disturbingly, he was finding himself wanting to more than "keep her company." He wanted the opportunity to not even let her out of his sight—for the next twenty-four hours, at least.

The guy who'd tossed Carrie away just as cavalierly as Alexia had thrown his ring in the pool had been a total imbecile. The sweat dribbled down Mike's open shirt collar and pooled, damn it, somewhere near his navel. Without even trying, the woman set him virtually on fire. And here she was saying she was about to leave?

Carrie tapped her toe against the pool deck and considered his disappointingly not-so-indecent proposal. Forgetting the drop-dead gorgeous part, he did appear to be a very nice guy. Maybe even nice enough to be her friend. Which would be a definite first for Carrie St. John, as she'd never befriended any man for longer than thirty-six hours without things between them becoming intimate. But, of course, as her track record consisted only of two serious beaus, maybe she was being a bit hasty in making a sweeping assessment.

Besides, friendship was good. Perhaps even what she most needed at the moment. And having a friend who looked and carried himself like the athletically inclined Mike Davis, could quite possibly come in handy. Maybe even in the very near future.

"All right, I'll stay," Carrie said, "but under one condition."

"Any condition's fine with me," Mike said, knowing that as long as whatever it was involved his taking off his boiling clothes, it would be A-OK with him. Particularly if it involved Carrie St. John stripping down as well.

"You understand this thing between us is about camaraderie. Two down-and-outs on the same flip side of the coin. Compadres."

Mike gave her a tight smile, damning every inner instinct he had and telling his licentious libido to behave. "Sure thing, Carrie," he said, reaching out an arm to shake her hand. "We'll play it any way you want."

****

Chapter Three

Carrie sat in the narrow oaken stairwell, finally getting a cell signal. The remoteness of the inn made service unpredictable. Carrie hadn't been able to pick up more than two bars anywhere but here.

She nervously twirled a lock of chestnut hair, rehearsing what she would tell her grandmother. *I'm sorry, Grandmother, but things just didn't work out…* No, Carrie had already been there and done that one. Besides, her second strike would make her look like a total washout, not the "together" young woman her adoring Grandma Russell took her to be.

Grandmother, there's been a last-minute change in plans…

Nope, that would only make her look inconsiderate. Horribly inconsiderate, given the wedding shower was scheduled for tomorrow.

Carrie sighed and hit autodial, trusting something brilliant would come to mind the instant she heard her grandmother's voice.

"Hello?"

"Grandmother, it's Carrie—"

"Oh, sweetheart," her grandma began in her endless prattle, "so lovely to hear your voice. Amelia and I were just discussing china patterns, and we really think the one you—"

"Grandmother…"

"Oh, lands sakes, child. I know, I know! Really none of my business. But, to tell you the truth, the everyday pattern you picked is ever so much more attractive and could really double for formal ware if push came to shove, and—"

Carrie blew a hard breath. This was going to be even harder than she'd imagined. "Grandmother!"

"Well, okay, okay, dear. You are absolutely right about that! Who needs to fret over china patterns when you've got a perfectly gorgeous man on your arm!"

"Grandma Russell!" Carrie shouted into the phone.

"Well, gracious me, child, you don't need to yell. Ma Bell's improved quite a bit since the days I courted your grandpa." She chuckled. "Lands sakes, child. Meant that one the other way around—quite the other way…"

Carrie sighed and slumped back against the wall behind her.

"Now, sweetheart," her grandmother finally asked, "what was it you wanted to tell me?"

Carrie racked her brain for a creative intro. "Well, it's about seating arrangements, actually."

"Tomorrow, sweetie? Your great-aunties and I've got that all worked out. No need for you to fret one bit. Nellie even hand-stitched the place cards."

The bottom dropped out of Carrie's stomach. "Aunt Nellie crocheted those beautiful lace place cards? But, I thought… That was supposed to be part of her wedding gift! I thought she was making those for the…wedding."

"Couldn't wait to see your face, she said. And you'll have to really butter her up on this one too, sweetness. She did a divine job. Absolutely divine! You would think the royal family was coming to tea, and not just your wedding party."

Carrie swallowed hard and tried to summon her courage. "Grandma…?"

"Yes, dearie?"

"What time is the shower again?"

"Land sakes, child, you are a nervous bride, aren't you? Four o'clock, same as it was last time you asked. But don't worry if you're not here right on the button. Just don't make us old gals wait too long. You know how it is with us geriatrics. We tend to nod off after a while when nothing's happening!"

"Don't worry, Grandma," Carrie said. "I promise not to put anybody to sleep."

Grandma Russell chuckled. "From what you've told me, you and that handsome groom of yours will be sure to wake up any crowd!"

"Right," Carrie agreed, feeling the fire of deceit spread from her temples to her collarbone.

"Can't wait to see what he looks like, dearie," Grandma Russell crooned into the phone. "Me and the girls have been speculating all day."

"That makes two of us," Carrie said quietly, ending the call.

"What's that?" Mike asked from the landing.

Carrie looked up, startled. "Oh, Mike, I didn't hear you come in."

"No?" he asked. "Could have sworn you said something about the two of—"

"Oh no," Carrie said with a blush. "That was my grandmother. Just got off the phone with her about..."

"Some of those plans that needed canceling?" Mike ventured.

Carrie gave him a shaky smile. "More or less."

"Say, you all right?" he asked, taking the steps two at a time and coming up to where she sat trembling at the bend in the stairs. "Because to tell you the truth, Carrie, you don't look so hot."

"Bet you say that to all the girls," she said, twisting her lips into the best imitation of a smile she could muster.

"Actually," he told her, "it's just the opposite."

"Now I see why you're not married."

Mike crossed his arms over his chest and leaned a shoulder against the wall. "This has something to do with Wilson, doesn't it?"

Carrie vehemently shook her head as moisture brimmed in her eyes.

Mike cocked his chin and scrutinized her.

"Okay," she admitted, making an inch-wide motion with her thumb and forefinger. "Maybe a little…"

Mike shook his head and held his ground.

"All right already! More than a little bit, okay? What is it exactly you want me to say?" she asked as coal-hot tears streamed down her cheeks. "That my life is a total mess? That everyone in my hometown is expecting me to show up for a bridal shower tomorrow—with my groom-to-be—and my groom-to-be has dumped me for a woman with a better financial portfolio?"

Mike dropped down on the step beside her and draped a steadying arm around her trembling shoulders.

"You don't have to be nice to me," she asserted, trying her damndest to set her jaw but failing miserably.

"I know," Mike said, reaching over and raising her chin. "But I want to be."

"But why?" Carrie asked with a sniff. "What could possibly be in it for you? I've already told you I want nothing more than…"

"Carrie, I have a question," Mike said, searching her bleary eyes.

"About what?"

"The people at this shower. Do they know…? I mean, have any of them actually met Wilson?"

"Well, only Paulette. But that was over a year ago."

"So then, she might not notice if Wilson has changed a bit? Lost some weight? Shaved his beard?"

"Lost some weight? What in the world are you talking about? Wilson was—and always will be—the ultimate bean pole! And he never had a beard!"

Carrie stared in amazement as Mike's lips curved into a devilish smile. Though, in truth, the thought had crossed her own mind once or twice—she'd never envisioned the absurd notion becoming a reality.

"Wait a minute! You couldn't possibly be thinking… That you—"

Mike nodded. "Darling, I've waited forever to meet your family."

Carrie straightened under the weight of his arm. "Very funny."

"I wasn't joking."

Carrie looked him square in the eye. "But you can't be serious! Why ever on earth would you do that for me?"

"To buy you some time?" he said, giving her shoulders a light squeeze. "Hey, I know firsthand how disorienting this type of situation can be. The last thing a nice girl like you needs is having to face her family with the abysmal news—when you alone haven't even adjusted to it yourself."

Carrie wriggled out from under his arm and set aside the cell phone. "Who says I haven't adjusted?"

Mike raised his brow and trailed a finger down her tearstained cheek. "Wild guess?"

Carrie dropped her head. "I would never accept an offer like that from a stranger." Even one who sent her stomach all aflutter like him, Carrie told herself. "Particularly not knowing you well enough to really know what you expect in return."

"No problem. I can tell you that."

Carrie looked up and arched both eyebrows. "Class of Ninety-two."

****

Chapter Four

"The plan is impossible," Carrie said, stabbing into her salad with her fork.

"Improbable, maybe," Mike said, biting into his burger. "Nothing is impossible."

"But you're talking about walking into a big group of my relatives and friends and convincing them we've been an item for—what?—a year and a half now? They'll see through it in an instant."

"Not if we're convincing," Mike said, shaking his head. He set down his burger and picked up his bottle of imported beer. "Besides, how much do these people really know about Wilson Haywood anyway? You said the two of you met in New York."

"We did."

"That your relationship was mainly on weekends."

"It was."

"Sometimes there, sometimes here—right in quaint little Mill Creek."

"What, precisely, is your point?" Carrie asked, sipping her iced tea.

"My point," Mike said, taking a swig of beer, "is that your relationship with Wilson wasn't exactly...normal."

"Oh, and you're such an expert on normal relationships," she pointed out with a broad sweep of her knife.

Mike bolted backward in his chair. "Watch it with that thing! Don't slay the messenger. I'm just telling it like it is. People don't see you all touchy-feely with your fiancé, they might figure, well, that's just a product of how things developed."

Carrie took exception to what he was suggesting. On the one hand, he might just be trying to save her some trouble by playing things cool like she wanted. On the other, he might very well be insinuating that Carrie was a cold fish. Which she certainly was not. And clearly wouldn't be with a man like Mike Davis standing beside her.

"And if things were 'touchy-feely,' as you put it, between me and Wilson?"

"Were they?" Mike asked, little crinkles tugging at the corners of his sea-green eyes.

Carrie put down her knife and thought about that. The truth was, no. Wilson had been very businesslike in a number of things, including in his relationship with her. She'd even sworn he'd timed their lovemaking so as to be less disruptive of the professional calls he'd always placed before—and afterward.

"Well?" Mike pressed, his honey complexion taking on a deeper hue that perfectly complemented his rugged appeal. It was hard to picture him in real estate, when the word outdoorsman was written all over his chiseled face. Not to mention his hard-toned body.

"Well, if you must know," Carrie began, feeling the slightest bit naughty but not the least bit ashamed of her duplicity. "Wilson was quite an affectionate man."

Mike choked on his pickle. "That so?"

"Oh yes," Carrie said, putting on her most confidential face. "It was somewhat embarrassing actually. PDA to the max! Sometimes, I practically had to beat him off with a stick!"

"A stick?" Mike gave up on his pickle and took a long drag of beer. "That doesn't mean you'll be hurting me, does it?"

"Not in the least," Carrie assured him, feeling a familiar ache wend its way all the way down to her bones. An ache that told her she was going to enjoy this little party a lot more than she'd originally suspected.

"Ah darn," Mike said with a Cheshire-cat grin. "But, no worries. We can work around that."

"You just remember your mission," Carrie cautioned him sternly, again with the knife.

"Anything you say, oh knife-wielding one."

Carrie laughed and looked down at her hand. "No cracking jokes at the shower. Got it? Especially none that would give the two of us away."

"Your wish is my command."

Carrie wondered about that. Wondered, especially, if she'd been just a tad bit rash in insisting this thing between her and Mike remain simply "friends."

"You're awfully quiet," Mike said, cocking one eyebrow. "Thinking up those three wishes?"

But, honestly, Carrie only found herself thinking of one. About how nice it would have been if Wilson had been a bit more like Mike. More relaxed and easy to get along with.

"It's funny, really," she admitted over the rim of her tinkling glass, "but I was thinking about how different you are from Wilson."

Mike settled back in his chair. "And that—at this precise moment in time—would be a compliment?"

Carrie smiled and set down her glass. "You're a nice man, Mike Davis."

"Ah-ah," he said, shaking his head. "Please don't tell me that!"

"That you're nice? Why ever on earth not?"

Mike coughed and picked up his beer. "Let's just say that the only woman who's ever called me nice and is still talking to me is my second-grade teacher, Mrs. Rich."

"Let me guess," Carrie said, narrowing her eyes. "Alexia said you were too nice for her."

"Bingo," Mike said, setting down his empty beer. "Ditto that, Carol. And Marianne, and Barbara…"

"My, my," Carrie said, pursing her lips. "You do have quite a reputation, don't you?"

"As the perpetual bachelor, yes," he said with a frown.

"But that's a reputation most men would savor."

"Well, if you haven't noticed, I'm not most men."

Oh, she'd noticed all right. Noticed in a heartbeat. "So what exactly is it that you're after, nice-guy Mike Davis?" she asked with a teasing smile. "If it's not your personal freedom, like most men."

"I've had my personal freedom," he assured her. "So much of it, I'm practically drowning in it. But to answer your question—"

"Honestly," she said, laying her napkin on the table, "all kidding aside."

"Honestly? Don't you think it's a bit risky to be asking honesty of a man you met less than a day ago?"

"No more risky than taking him home to meet my grandmother."

Mike gave her a broad, sweeping smile that settled into an affectionate grin. "Ah Carrie, you're really very sweet."

"Now, don't go calling me sweet—"

Mike chortled. "Let me guess? Something like my Mr. Nice Guy?"

Carrie felt the heat envelope her at the thought of being read so easily. But he could read her easily, this man she scarcely knew. Or perhaps it was simply because the two of them were in the same boat that he happened to know exactly what she was feeling, precisely when she was feeling it.

"Okay," Mike continued, "to answer your question—honestly. What I'm after is probably not so different from what you are. A stable relationship, a home. Kids, maybe."

"A white picket fence?" she asked, feeling the renewed heat in her cheeks.

"Sure, why not? If you can get one of those in the Caymans," he added with a grin.

Carrie's heart fell a million miles. What on earth had she been thinking? Kidding herself about a potential relationship with someone she'd met in such a haphazard manner? Hoping against hope that taking him home as the man of her dreams would somehow convert him to that before her very eyes? *Come on, now, Carrie, wake up—and join the twenty-first century!*

Besides, the man was already making plans to move to the Caymans. More than a stone's throw from Virginia. This little charade between them involving her shower and his reunion next weekend was all she had. And Carrie St. John and her woebegone heart would do very well to remember that.

Mike took a running dive into the crystal clear waters of the pool, thinking that things weren't going quite as swimmingly with Carrie St. John as he'd planned. He was glad she'd agreed to go to his reunion. More than glad—ecstatic, actually—that a stunning woman like her would help him save face with his friends. And he didn't mind stepping into Wilson's shoes for her bridal shower one bit. What bothered him was the make-believe element to their whole affair. It was definitely a screwy way to begin a relationship. Non-relationship, he reminded himself, as per Carrie's instructions.

For anybody else, it would have been the perfect setup. He'd make out like a bandit at his high school reunion—no strings attached. But, for Mike, who felt an inexplicable yearning to stay by Carrie's side in a much more than fraternal fashion, the whole picture rotted—big-time.

Plus, it really seemed like an unfair trade. Carrie's shower, after all, was only a mere couple of hours out of one afternoon. His reunion, on the other hand, was an entire weekend-long extravaganza. Of course, he hadn't quite told her that—yet. But he would. Just not until after she'd been sufficiently impressed with the way he'd wowed her family and friends. Then, she'd feel beholden—at least in some small way—and would still agree to come to his rescue. Even if it involved a fancy dinner and a Sunday afternoon picnic.

Yeesh! This was where having gone to a private school most definitely paid. Nothing that Ashton Academy did was anything less than first-class. And Carrie St. John was definitely a first-class kind of girl. Mike would be the envy of every man in that room, he thought with a smile as he stroked his way across the pool. Heck, if only it weren't such a big illusion, he'd even be the envy of his own former self!

Carrie turned in the mirror and studied the cellulite on her thighs. What had she been thinking? Telling Mike she might possibly join him for a swim? These thunder thighs weren't going anywhere except for maybe into a pair of shorts. A pair of very long, very modestly proportioned shorts, Carrie thought, rifling through her suitcase.

But if Mike was supposedly nothing more than a friend, what was she all hellfire worried about? Friends didn't dump friends over a pair of weighty thighs.

Friendship was based on other things, like mutual respect. Common interests and goals…

Carrie sat heavily on the bed. She certainly hadn't known Mike long enough to get a handle on the interests part, but she and the "swim god" definitely shared common goals. Though she hadn't dared tell him so, the ideal he was after wasn't really so far from her own. Except for the Cayman Islands part. The Caymans! Ironically enough, an investor's heaven. One of her business associates in New York had been pressing Carrie to open up a bank there for almost a decade. But Carrie had always preferred to channel her funds into more personal ventures. It was helping out entrepreneurs that gave her the most satisfaction. Small businesses, start-up operations like this country inn here.

Then again, the Caymans did hold possibilities… Not the least of which stood about six foot two and had the perfect smattering of dark blond hair on its chest.

Carrie walked to the bathroom and threw some cold water on her face. She was losing her mind! Losing it completely! Actually considering the notion…

Now, for a vacation, maybe.

Carrie smiled into the mirror at visions of her and a very oiled-up Mike Davis stretched out on a white-sand beach.

But that idea was ludicrous too! She and Mike didn't stand a prayer of a chance starting out the way they had. Besides, the two of them had made a pact. And, despite his occasional flirtation which Carrie assumed was second nature to a man like him, he truthfully didn't seem interested in being more than just friends. All Mike was after was a way to impress his old high school buddies. But returning to the full-length mirror and studying her silhouette once again, Carrie was uncertain why he imagined she could do the trick. Though Carrie considered herself reasonably attractive, she was well aware she had what the magazines called "figure flaws." Flaws that Wilson had occasionally been unkind enough to point out—in his own teasing way. A way which Carrie hadn't found the least bit amusing.

Maybe she'd just slip on the denim shorts and stroll on down to the pool. It would look odd if she failed to show completely. And she certainly didn't want Mike thinking she was nervous about facing him. Though she was. Utterly nervous. Mostly because, when she saw the man half-nude, her thoughts ran wild. Straight into the "Mike, Tarzan; Carrie, Jane" jungle! And now that she figured him to be a nice guy on top of the way he looked... Well, Carrie wasn't quite sure she could trust her own reaction.

She'd heard of people on the rebound. The rampant bed-hopping that sometimes went on when one wounded partner was getting over the other. But Carrie had never figured herself to be the bed-hopping type. In fact, before Wilson, there'd really only been one other man. The first one she'd thought she would marry and, soon after their break-up, had started referring to as "old what's-his-name."

But even "old what's-his-name," her first lover ever, hadn't stirred her half as much as Mike Davis. But maybe that was what she got for comparing twenty-two-year-old apples to thirty-something-year-old oranges. Very ripe, very succulent oranges. Criminy!

Carrie sighed and hunted for a belt that would do her waistline justice—meaning suck it in just a tad more than its natural state. Though, of course, a friend wouldn't notice her waistline one way or another, she told herself, sweeping her hair into a ponytail and arranging her tresses in the mirror. Friends didn't care what friends looked like, just as long as they kept their word.

Mike's eyes popped open when he heard the clack of sandal heels on the pavement. Carrie St. John headed down the path in strappy black sandals, a formfitting tee and cuffed denim shorts. She certainly was revealing a lot more flesh than she had been earlier, but not nearly enough for Mike's satisfaction, he thought, sitting up to disguise his reaction that would have been otherwise quite evident through his swim shorts.

"You're not swimming?"

"Can't," she said with a congenial smile. "Still got lots of telephone calls."

A buzz of panic shot to Mike's brain. "But I thought we—"

"Oh yes... I mean, no." She blew a soft breath that sent a loose tendril spiraling. "I'm not backing out of our deal or anything like that."

Mike sat back against the lounge chair, relieved. He'd actually been looking forward to playing Carrie's fiancé. Especially, he thought, eying her well-formed bosom through her unforgiving cotton top, once he'd learned about that touchy-feely part.

"It's just that I've still got a lot of calls to make, and I want to try to catch the businesses while they're still open."

Mike raised his eyebrows.

"Flower shops, the caterer... You would not believe all that goes into a wedding!"

"No." Mike gave her a melancholy smile. "Guess I've never gotten that far."

"Oh, sorry," Carrie said, bringing her hands to her flaming cheeks. "Didn't mean to make you feel bad."

Actually, Mike thought, Carrie did a pretty fine job of making him feel terrific. "It's all right," he assured her.

"But I thought you weren't going to cancel those things until after the shower?"

"The sooner, the better," she told him. "Unless I want to get stuck footing the bill for a wedding that doesn't happen.

"You're really sweet to agree to be my fiancé tomorrow. Really very sweet. You were absolutely right; I needed to buy myself some time. Once I've taken care of canceling the other arrangements and smoothing out all the wrinkles, breaking the news to my family won't be as hard."

"Glad I could help," Mike said, feeling as if he should stand but still not exactly trusting what his body was doing. Carrie St. John had an unusual effect on him. Though she was certainly not the most beautiful woman he'd ever seen, she was definitely one of the most womanly. There was something very sensual about the way her feminine curves suited her just right. Curves he found himself itching to get his hands around.

"Gonna cool off," Mike said, startling Carrie by bolting to his feet and diving in a split-second lunge into the pool.

"Fine!" Carrie called after him as he popped his head above the water. "I'll be back at the inn. Maybe we can meet for dinner and plan out tomorrow?"

"Absolutely!" Mike called after her before dunking his steaming head back under the surface.

****

Chapter Five

Carrie dropped down on all fours and searched the oriental carpet for the back of her earring. This was ridiculous. Really! Five minutes until dinner and Carrie was quaking in her sandals like a nervous teenager. You would think this was her first date and not a mere business arrangement with a friend.

And that's strictly what it is, she thought, finally locating the jewelry piece and standing to insert her earring in the mirror. Strictly business. She and Mike Davis had made a deal, a pact to help each other out in this uncanny time of distress for the two of them. He would butter up her family, and she, in turn, would schmooze with his prep school cronies. Next weekend would be over before she knew it, and her loosely knotted affiliation with Mike Davis would be over altogether.

Carrie frowned at her reflection, wondering what would have become of her and Mike Davis if Mike had truly occupied Wilson's slot all this while. Of course, she wouldn't have met Mike in New York, but then, as he lived closer, perhaps their relationship would have been better maintained than her and Wilson's weekend-style affair.

Carrie watched herself color at the thought of maintaining any kind of affair with the hunky Mike Davis. Criminy. Blushing like a schoolgirl, and he wasn't even in the room!

Mike tossed his Polo shirt onto the bed, thinking it was really too damn preppy. Not only that, he reminded himself, at this sort of place, one had to wear a tie.

Mike walked over and thumbed through the hanging clothes in the mirrored armoire that served as his closet. A sports coat and light starch button-down would work. That and his conservative yellow—no, too Wall Street, he told himself. He certainly couldn't have Carrie thinking stockbrokers on a night like this.

Although it was true Mike was out to impersonate Wilson, he was just as determined to prove to Carrie just how different from Wilson he actually was. Because, like it or not, in less than a day, the voluptuous Carrie St. John had gotten right under Mike Davis's skin. He didn't know how it'd happened. Or even how in the world she'd done it. Particularly since—from the get-go—she'd seemed so determined to keep this arrangement between them strictly friends.

Oh, Mike could get friendly with Carrie, all right. More than friendly. Downright carnal, in fact. But the puzzling thing was, Mike's growing attraction to Carrie involved more than just hormones. There was something about her. Something very earthy and real that set her miles apart from plastic, poised women like Alexia.

Carrie was pretty, all right. No one could argue that point. But what made her truly beautiful was that—unlike Alexia, who'd been attractive in a more Seventh Avenue way—she didn't appear to know it. Yet, there was something very womanly about her. Something so soft and feminine it made Mike ache to be all man. Christ, he thought, looking down at his boxers. Only three minutes till eight, and he'd have to take another cold shower.

Carrie sat alone at the romantic outdoor cafe table. All around her, other couples dined, trading secrets in hushed whispers, many of them linking hands.

This inn was the perfect lovers' retreat…assuming the lovers were still together, she sighed. Well, maybe her grandmother was right. Ever since she'd been a little girl, Grandma Russell, who had raised her, had insisted that things always turned out for the best. And maybe finding out Wilson was a two-timing jerk was best done now—and not after the wedding.

The maître d' appeared and offered to pour her wine, but she told him she'd wait. Carrie checked her watch and saw it was ten after eight. Terror flashed through her. What if Mike had deserted her too? What if, despite her initial impression, he turned out to be just as gutless as Wilson and had—at the last minute—ridden off into the sunset, leaving her to face her grandmother, great-aunts, and friends all on her own?

Carrie noticed a dignified older gentleman standing near the door that led to the inn's kitchen engaged in conversation with the maître d'. The silver-haired man, whom Carrie guessed to be in his late sixties, stroked his goatee, then sent Carrie a warming smile across the nest of tables that separated them.

He must be the innkeeper, she thought, taking a sip of water. But before she could set down her glass, he approached and extended his hand. "Ms. St. John," he said with a genuine smile, "Charles Gilpatrick. I wanted to tell you what a pleasure it is to have you at our inn. I would have spoken with you yesterday evening but have just now returned from an innkeepers' conference in Roanoke."

Carrie gave his hand a firm squeeze and smiled back at him. "I'm so glad you came over to say hello. You've done a remarkable job with the inn. It's beautiful."

"And suited to your taste, I trust?" he asked, releasing his grip. "We can't have our chief financier unhappy with the accommodations."

Carrie felt her cheeks warm at the compliment but held a single finger to her lips. "Let's just keep that our little secret," she said with a wink. "I don't get away on vacation that often, and when I do—"

"Yes, of course. I realize how difficult it must be for you not to be bothered. You are probably one of the more successful investors of our time."

"You do go on!" she said with a laugh.

"Well, any woman who makes the cover of *Forbes* by age twenty-six…"

Carrie shushed him with a shake of her head. "When I'm in Virginia, Mr. Gilpatrick—"

"Please, call me Charles."

Carrie smiled up at the ingratiating older man. "Charles. While in investment circles I may be known for my financial acumen…" A modest, self-deprecating laugh. "In Virginia, I prefer to simply be known as Carrie."

"But of course," Charles said, extending his grip to seal their agreement. "The girl next door. Not a problem, Ms. St John."

"Carrie," she corrected, graciously accepting his lingering handshake. "And I thank you for your discretion."

Charles lifted her hand lightly to his lips and gave the back of it a deft kiss.

"Will your fiancé be joining you for dinner?" Charles asked, straightening. "I understand his name was on the register."

"He'll be here any minute," Carrie said in an effort to reassure herself just as much as the innkeeper. Where on earth could he possibly be? Women were supposed to be the tardy ones. And clearly that was understandable, what with all the primping and trouble that went into sliding on control-top panty hose without running them silly. But Mike Davis was strictly wash-and-wear. Carrie was certain he'd look just as good stepping out of a shower as he had coming out of the pool. What was keeping that infuriating man?

Mike froze in his tracks, unable to believe what he was seeing. Who was that old goat sending his roving eyes all over Carrie's plunging neckline? And why was she laughing and tossing back her head in that coquettish fashion that said whatever he was telling her really floated her boat?

Mike blew a hard breath and ran his fingers through his hair, thinking he was probably blowing things all out of proportion. That couldn't be Wilson, could it? Come back to claim his bride? The man was old enough to be her father!

Carrie turned her head in Mike's direction, and he ducked back behind the fanning leaves of a potted fern. Mike needed to really think this thing out. Maybe if he asked one of the waiters…

Mike jumped a mile high when he felt the feminine touch at his forearm.

"Not going to find me in there," Carrie said, motioning to the spreading fern.

"No, of course not," Mike said. "I just dropped a…" Well, as he wasn't wearing a tux, he certainly couldn't say cufflink.

"An engagement ring?" Carrie questioned with a teasing smile.

"Why, no. No… A pen."

"Right," Carrie deadpanned.

Mike's brow shot up. "Pen? Ha-ha! I said pen, didn't I? No, I actually meant—"

Carrie twisted her lips and studied the color sweeping up his neckline. Mike hadn't dropped a darn thing into that planter. He'd been spying on her!

"Well, look, if it isn't the Hope Diamond you've dropped in that dirt, how about you forget about it for now and come on over to the table. There's someone there I'd like you to meet."

Mike looked her up and down and swallowed hard. God, was she gorgeous in that long black dress. It was simple but elegant, just like her. "Oh?" Mike asked, clearing his throat. "Friend of yours? Old...friend?"

Carrie held back a laugh at his curious expression. She couldn't decide if his color was more eggplant or pomegranate. But why? Over Charles Gilpatrick?

"Why, yes. I suppose you could say that. At least you've got it half right."

Darn it. Mike knew it! Half right meaning he'd been correct about the old part. Clearly Wilson would no longer be Carrie's friend. But why, then, had she been carrying on in such a flirtatious fashion? Encouraging the geezer, who was, holy cow, old enough to be her father! When he'd agreed to pose as Carrie's fiancé, she hadn't told him he'd have to dust his head with baby powder!

"Listen, Carrie, I don't know if now is the time..."

But she'd already latched on to his arm and was dragging him toward her table. "No time like the present."

The white-haired gentleman stuck out his arm. "Wilson Haywood, I presume."

Mike firmly gripped his hand, slam-dunked by the realisation. Hey, whoa! It took every ounce of restraint Mike had not to thumb his chest like an idiot and say, *"Who, me?"*

He shot a quick glance at Carrie, who slipped him a sly wink. Oh, so it was showtime, was it? A little practicing up for his big debut? Yeesh! The least Carrie could have done was warn him. Well, now, maybe it was her turn to be caught off guard.

Mike gave the older man's hand a firm squeeze. "Indeed it is. And, you…?"

"Sweetheart," Carrie said, beaming a bit too radiantly, in Mike's opinion. "This is Charles Gilpatrick, the innkeeper here."

Mike's chest wall relaxed a notch. Of course he was the innkeeper. Who on earth else could he have been?

"I trust," Mr. Gilpatrick said, directing his question at Mike, "you and Ms. St. John are enjoying your stay here?"

Mike stepped over and drew a tight arm around Carrie's shoulders. "Delightful place. You should be very proud of what you've done with it. You've only been in business for about a year now, isn't that right?"

Gilpatrick's gray eyes warmed in appreciation. "I see Carrie's not the only one with an aptitude for doing her homework."

Mike pulled Carrie in a little tighter, her side heating his skin, even through his clothing. "She's quite the student, my Carrie," Mike said, caressing her shoulder.

Carrie squirmed in his grip as his fire spiked through her. It started at his fingertips, where they lightly massaged and caressed her bare shoulder, ricocheted to her breastbone, then sank low in her belly. Boy, was she done for, Carrie thought, realizing she'd missed something in the conversation and that both Charles and Mike now had their expectant gazes turned on her.

"Honey?" Mike asked, leaning over, his whiskey whisper tickling her ear.

Carrie blanched, suddenly light-headed. "Yeah, sure. That's fine," she responded, sinking into her chair beneath the two men's congenial laughter.

"The Merlot will be fine, Charles," Mike said. "Thanks so much for the offer and coming over to introduce yourself."

"The pleasure's all mine," Charles said, departing with a nod of his head.

Carrie picked up her water glass and drained most of it while Mike sat across from her. "What was so funny?" she asked, knowing she'd embarrass herself by asking but fearing it would be worse for her still if she never even knew.

Mike's smile broadened over his own water glass. "Charles had offered a complimentary bottle of Virginia wine, or in your case, since you're such a special guest—his entire wine cellar, to which you—"

Carrie rested her near-empty water glass against the side of her flaming cheek. "Indicated I'd take the whole wine cellar."

"More or less," Mike replied with a grin. "But, no worries, I saved our new friend from bankruptcy by agreeing to take him up on his earlier offer of a Merlot instead."

"I see," said Carrie, setting down her glass.

A wine steward appeared and displayed a Norton Vineyard label before Mike. "Excellent year," Mike said. "Believe that one was an award winner, wasn't it?"

Their server nodded solemnly and uncorked the bottle with white-gloved hands. After a brief wine-tasting interlude, the beverage was poured and Mike and Carrie left alone to once again confront each other in peace.

"Mind telling me why we are considered such special guests in this place?" Mike asked, lifting his glass.

"Mind telling me how you know so much about Virginia wines?"

Mike swirled his glass and surveyed the softly shadowed face of the woman in front of him. Elegant, sophisticated, and, if she was getting special treatment from innkeepers, most likely rich. In light of all that, Mike somehow didn't think telling Carrie he'd spent his high school summers working the vineyards would sound all that impressive.

"Let's just say," Mike said, lightly clinking her glass, "I'm a man of impeccable taste."

"To impeccable taste," Carrie said, raising her wine to her lips.

"Seriously, Carrie," Mike said, once they'd both set their glasses back on the table. "Why is it that we, or rather you, merit such special treatment here?"

Carrie looked at him innocently and shrugged, picking up her menu.

Mike reached out and lowered the laminated page so he could look in her eyes. "Are you...? You're not...?"

"What?" she asked, her eyes lighting with amusement. "Somebody famous?"

Mike leaned in just a tiny bit more. "We-ell?" he asked, drawing out the word in a blood-pounding way as sea-green eyes washed all over her.

Carrie laid down her menu and gripped the table edge to get her bearings. "Nope. Nobody famous, if you must know. Just your regular old girl from Virginia. Hope that doesn't disappoint too much."

Uh-uh. Carrie St. John had done nothing to disappointment him yet, and she wasn't going to start now. Her eyes were fanning wide, half playful, half daring. The deepest chocolate brown, even darker by candlelight than they'd appeared in the light of day. And everything about her seemed to be drawing Mike closer. Even as he willed himself to remain stoic in his chair.

But instead of staying put, Mike found himself reaching across the table. Wrapping her satiny shoulders in his trembling grip, leaning his mouth in toward hers as the moonlight and the table and the milling voices of others all melted away.

Carrie tilted her chin in expectation and didn't break away. Rather than pause, she seemed susceptible to the same raging pull that had engulfed Mike's senses. Her eyes lingered tantalizingly on his own—beckoning, promising. She let out a little gasp, lightly moistening her lips.

"Ready to order?" the maître d' inquired, slicing the air between them.

"Not on your life," Mike said, slamming down his napkin.

****

Chapter Six

"Excuse me," Carrie said, abruptly pushing back her chair. "I'm going to powder my nose."

Thank God, Carrie could hear herself thinking. Thank God, thank God, thank God! If that maître d' hadn't interrupted just in the nick of time, who knew what would have happened?

Carrie knew exactly.

She pushed her way into the ladies room and made a beeline for the faucet, where she ran the water cold.

Get a grip, Carrie, she warned herself sternly, dousing some paper towels and dabbing them at her neckline and brow. Water streamed from her neck to cleavage, reminding her of the effect Mike Davis had inspired at the pool. What was it with this man and water! Every time Carrie thought of him…

Carrie looked up into the mirror and found her face a heated flush

And this was supposed to make things all better? Getting tangled up with someone new when her heart hadn't even had half a chance to heal was going to somehow alleviate the ache in her life?

Carrie shook her head at the woman in the mirror. Plain old girl from Virginia was right. To look at her now, no one would ever suspect her worldly sophistication. They'd liken her, in fact, to some high school hayseed, fallen right off the turnip truck.

Mike sat at the table, dumbfounded. This had to be the longest nose-powdering in history, he thought, staring down at his and Carrie's lukewarm entrees.

She'd agreed to let him place the orders, but then had bolted like a minnow in the path of a manta ray.

Mike racked his brain for something—anything—he could have done wrong, but all he came up with was that "almost" kiss. Now, if he had kissed her and botched it miserably, he would have understood her wanting to take flight. But he hadn't even gotten his chance. And, no matter what excuses she planned to offer to the contrary—and Mike was quite certain that was what she was doing at the moment, concocting excuses—there'd been that unmistakable look in her eye that said she'd wanted him to take it.

Mike had been with plenty of women, enough of them to know when one wanted kissing and wanted it badly. Was it really possible all his years of training could fail him now?

Mike stood from the table, thinking he should go check on her. As far as he knew, Carrie didn't own a black Jaguar to escape in, but Mike supposed it was possible that Carrie could decide to run out on him just as Alexia had.

Mike was just rounding the corner where trellised vines climbed heavenward when he ran smack into Carrie.

"I was just coming to check on you," he said when she halted in surprise.

"Sorry," she said with a trembling smile. "I had to collect myself."

"You doing all right?" Mike asked with concern.

Carrie looked at him, then pursed her lips to keep them steady.

"Carrie?"

Her eyes fell to the ground as she slowly shook her head. "It's no use, Mike," she said, her voice cracking up. "This whole charade is—"

"Who says it's all a charade?" Mike asked, stepping forward and taking her by the elbows.

"Mike," she said, looking up and trying her damndest to look tough. Be in control. But Mike could see Carrie St. John was no more in control of her own racing heart than he was of his. "This thing, this arrangement, simply isn't going to work."

"Says who?" he asked, stepping closer as a couple of departing diners scooted around them on the pathway. "Did you find that on some literature in the ladies'?"

Carrie heaved a sigh without smiling, but he could tell she was loosening up.

"Or perhaps," he said, sliding his arms around her waist and tugging her into his rock-solid frame, "you found something disparaging written about me on the bathroom walls?"

Carrie looked up at the impossible man and shook her head, trying to deflect the comfort of his humor, trying to make herself believe that nothing Mike Davis could say could possibly make things seem any better.

Mike reached out and tilted her chin. "None of it's true, Carrie," he said, his mouth closing in. "Except for maybe the part about me being a good time…"

Carrie's knees went weak at that thought, as his overpoweringly male scent washed over her in ocean waves.

Trying to fight her natural attraction to Mike Davis, she decided, was a losing battle.

And when he claimed her mouth with his, she knew it wasn't only battles they were talking. They were playing for the highest stakes. Every ounce of her hurting interior was at war with what her body was doing. Reveling in, encouraging, his bittersweet, luxurious kisses. Carrie wasn't even sure it was legal to kiss that well. Especially in the state of Virginia. Where exactly was that turnip truck, anyway? Carrie wondered, feeling herself spiral further and further away into the magic of Mike's embrace.

"Carrie," Mike said, pulling back, "maybe we ought to find someplace more private…"

A fanning burn in her throat prevented her from answering. She was hot and tipsy, his raging fire still tearing through her like the strongest scotch whiskey. And this was a drink she wanted straight up. No ice.

Mike bucked as the icy chill raced through his sports coat and centered in on his spine.

"Oh! Oh, my goodness!" the befuddled voice called behind him as a hard metallic clank echoed from somewhere near his feet. Cold water sloshed forward, followed by a parade of ice cubes. Mike whirled to find the red-faced young woman who'd just poured her champagne bucket down his back.

"Oh, gracious!" she continued to babble, kneeling to scoop the miraculously intact bottle of champagne of the brick walk. "I'm so sorry! Must have run straight into—"

From just over his shoulder, a woman erupted in raucous laughter.

Mike spun to find Carrie cupping a hand over her mouth as her whole upper body quaked with mirth.

If only he'd known what she'd been thinking! What was it about Mike Davis, Carrie wondered, that always seemed to attract him to water? Or vice versa, Carrie thought, exploding once again in giggles.

Mike ignored the woman at his feet, busily scooping ice cubes back into her silver bucket, and kept a watchful eye on Carrie as he stealthily removed his dripping sports coat and shook it out at arm's length.

"Feeling all better, I see," he said, cocking one eyebrow and looking— what? Carrie wondered—amused at her amusement?

"Sir, I—"

"Don't worry about it," Mike said, nearly deaf to the stranger's apologies as he stooped to gather ice cubes and toss the cleaner ones back into the bucket. "Accidents happen." But what had happened between him and Carrie just now hadn't been an accident at all. For the briefest moment, she'd been all his. And it had been wonderful. So wonderful he'd been itching to continue things on an even more intimate level back in his room. And now—this.

Finally, their embarrassed interloper straightened and made off with her champagne. Carrie, Mike noticed, still looked as if she was going to burst into hysterics at any moment.

"I—" She sputtered a laugh, then stopped and collected herself. "I am feeling much better, thank you. But you're— all wet…"

"Nothing that I haven't been before," he assured her, holding up his jacket to examine it in the moonlight. "I'm sure my clothing and I will survive."

To her embarrassment, Carrie's stomach growled loudly.

"Still hungry?" Mike asked, feeling for the ice cube that had wedged itself between his belt and waistband at the small of his back and plucking it free.

Carrie giggled again as he offered it as further proof of his ordeal.

Carrie lifted the ice cube from his palm and hurled it into the darkness. "Starved. But how about you? Don't you think you'd better, uh…change?"

"Change?" Mike grinned. "Thought you were starting to like me just the way I am."

Carrie felt herself color from head to toe. "You, Mike Davis, are—"

He cocked one eyebrow and waited.

"—a very nice man," she finished, feeling renewed heat in her cheeks.

Mike chuckled and brought a tender hand to her face. "Ah, Carrie. Yes. And you, my dear, are very—sweet."

Mike leaned forward and kissed her lightly on the forehead, something akin to affection sparkling in his eyes. No man had ever looked at Carrie like that before. With hunger, anticipation, yes. But this was a different sort of appreciation altogether, and it warmed her through and through.

"Want to see if dinner's still on the table?" he asked, taking her hand.

"Great idea," Carrie said, wondering what on earth was happening to her. This wasn't love. At least, not like she'd ever known it. Carrie St. John was falling "in like" with a man who looked like a god, and neither her heart nor her head knew precisely what to make of that.

****

Chapter Seven

Mike draped his still-damp clothing over the wooden hangers he'd suspended from the shower bar. All in all, things hadn't gone badly. Even if he had taken a bath, in a manner of speaking, the look on Carrie's face had been worth every ounce of icy discomfort. Somehow, Mike suspected, Carrie didn't get the opportunity for laughs often. Though laughter suited her beautifully. So well, in fact, Mike was going to make it his personal ambition to ensure she wore it more often.

Mike puzzled at his instant attraction to the woman he'd met a day ago. Yet, somehow, when he looked in her deep-brown eyes, he had the notion he'd known her a lifetime.

Now he was getting sappy, Mike thought, sitting down on the bed to tug off his socks. Thinking that things between him and Carrie had, in some way, been preordained. Just who did he think he was kidding? Mike's judgment in the past regarding women had left much to be desired. And yet, what he desired more than anything was a chance to prove—to himself and Carrie—that perhaps this time his instincts were dead-on.

There was something about her that got to him on more than just a physical level. He liked Carrie. Honestly enjoyed spending time with her. And, looking back, Mike wasn't sure he could make that unequivocal statement about any of the previous women in his life. Up until now, Mike had always looked at romance as a love/hate proposition. The woman you loved was supposed to drive you mad, wasn't she? Feminine wiles were supposed to be mysterious, impossible to understand. And, up until now,

Mike hadn't given one iota whether he'd understood them or not. Wooing women was something Mike had experience in. Plenty. But befriending them? That was a totally new concept altogether. And a woman who could prove both a lover and a friend...?

Mike fell back on the bed and pulled a fluffy pillow over his head. Maybe once he got down to the Caymans, he wouldn't have to deal with such bubbleheaded notions. A woman as a friend! Hoo! Who in Hades did he think he was fooling?

Carrie fluffed the pillow and repositioned it beneath her elbow, making believe she was reading the magazine. But truth be known, she'd been staring down at the same article on backyard decorating for the past twenty minutes and hadn't absorbed a thing.

The rest of the evening had gone like a charm. The two of them swapping humorous stories over their second bottle of complimentary Merlot. Though he'd had nothing to do with it personally, the innkeeper had been quite embarrassed by Mike's earlier run-in with the champagne bucket and had insisted on more wine as an apology.

Mike had accepted graciously, asking if it would be too much trouble to sample a different vintage, a sweet Virginia red perhaps, as they'd already moved on to dessert.

It still struck Carrie as odd that a realtor knew so much about wine. Not that he didn't have a right to be a connoisseur if he wanted. It was just that Carrie couldn't help the niggling sensation that something about Mike didn't add up.

He seemed so out of character as a realtor. And yet, if he professed that was what he did, what gave her reason to doubt him? Perhaps it was merely her own guilt seeping through. Guilt over not being completely honest with him about who she was or what she did. Though she'd informed him of the generalities, she'd very purposely ignored the particulars.

Mike seemed to like her so much, just as she was—the homespun girl from Virginia. And she, Carrie admitted truthfully, laying a palm over her fluttering heart, had been very much enjoying his down-to-earth, manly attentions. Finding out her net worth would surely change how he looked at her. And, at thirty-three, Carrie St. John had tired of being looked at as nothing more than a financial opportunity. Both of her boyfriends thus far, even the younger one in college, had seemed to sense she was going places and had wanted to latch on to her coattails. At least temporarily.

And that, probably, was why the romance had never lasted. No man had ever truly been attracted to who she was inside. No matter what her bank account said now, on the inside, Carrie was still the same simple girl who had sewn her dress from scratch in order to afford the prom.

But understanding her humble roots was not something even a nice man like Mike Davis could likely relate to. He, after all, had grown up in the lap of privilege himself. Ashton Academy cost more per year than Carrie's full university scholarship had provided per annum.

Carrie snapped off the light and sank back into the mattress, wondering just who she thought she was fooling. Mike was simply a nice man who had taken pity on her present circumstances. And no matter how badly her heart ached to be near him, it was high time Carrie started listening to her head. They were far too different from one another—she and Mike—to ever form anything long-lasting. She might as well just lie back and enjoy the temporary ride of having him in her life as her fiancé. From the looks of her life, it was as close to the real thing as Carrie would ever get.

"Ready to go?" Mike asked, standing in her open doorway. After a quick, cordial breakfast together, they'd each headed to their separate rooms to pack up.

He looked even better this morning than Carrie'd remembered, his well-tailored slacks and sports coat over open-collared shirt accentuating his exceptionally fit form. Carrie heaved a sigh, grateful, at least, for the dynamite impression he was going to make. But in some ways, having him wow her family was going to make it that much harder to disillusion them in the end. Somehow, she'd never considered that angle. Although it was definitely far too late to go having second thoughts now.

"Having second thoughts?" Mike asked, leaning forward and picking up her suitcase.

"Not at all," Carrie reported, fighting the fire in her cheeks. "Let's get started."

Mike took a cursory scan around the gravel parking area. "Your car or mine?"

Carrie cast a sideways glance at her shiny teal-blue BMW convertible. "Yours would be better, I think. Mine—needs work…"

"Oh?" Mike asked. "Maybe I can take a look at it. I'm pretty handy with cars, you know."

As far as Carrie was concerned, Mike seemed pretty handy with just about everything. "Uh, no. Thanks, I'll just take it to the shop when I get back."

"Seriously," Mike said, dropping the bags dangling at his sides to the ground. "Might be something really simple. I'd hate to think of you spending the—"

"Maybe when we get back," Carrie said, tugging at his elbow. "We really can't be late. My Grandma Russell would have a fit."

"Okay. Let me just put your suitcase in your car, then."

Carrie blew a hard breath and nervously latched on to a loose strand of hair. In all her boardroom negotiations, she'd never come across anything like this. Still, a very large part of her success had come from thinking on her feet.

"Actually," she said, motioning to her bag, "I've got some gifts in there for my aunts and grandmother. Too cumbersome to get it all out now."

Mike shrugged, seeming to buy that easily. "Oh, all right. I'll just toss it in my trunk, then."

Mike strode over to a late-model Mustang. Ancient but meticulously restored. Candy-apple red.

"Love the car," Carrie said, appreciatively patting the hood as Mike laid the bags in the trunk. "She's a real…" Carrie stopped short of saying "investment goldmine." "…beaut. You've done a great job with her."

"Thanks," Mike said, smiling as he came around to unlock Carrie's door. "I guess I do pretty well at taking care of the things that are important to me."

Carrie swallowed hard and stepped into the car without uttering a word. Did his words really carry the weight she thought he'd intended them to? No, Carrie, she admonished herself, don't be stupid. Get through this day, that's all. One day at a time. She'd think about the coming weekend, and Mike's reunion, and her miserable life afterward—tomorrow.

****

Chapter Eight

Paulette Pierce held out her narrow grip. "My, my, how time improves," she said, unabashedly looking Mike up and down. The moment they'd arrived, Carrie had been lost to a swirl of old ladies in pastel brocade, and Mike hadn't seen her since.

"Why thanks, Paulette," Mike said, shifting on his feet and taking her hand. The woman was birdlike and gaunt, probably Carrie's age, though her thinness made her appear much older. "I take that as a compliment."

Paulette enclosed his hand in her viselike flesh and leaned forward. "A compliment meant for you, not Wilson Haywood," she said in a hushed tone.

Mike fought the urge to wince in her talons and forced a tight smile.

Paulette kept hold of his hand and took a step forward, straight honey-colored hair swinging over her shoulders. "That stuffy old suit, Wilson," she continued in a whisper. "I can barely remember. But you, sweetheart, a gal's not likely to forget."

She leaned in and brought her mouth very close to his ear. "Is it serious?" she asked, just as Mike felt a hand on his shoulder.

"Paulette," Carrie said, stepping between the two of them. "How nice to see you getting reacquainted with Wilson." Carrie slipped an arm through one of Mike's and linked him in tight. "Isn't he even better than you remembered?"

"Quite," Paulette said, eyes narrowing. "In fact, if I didn't know better, I'd say—"

"Of course, the plastic surgery helped a lot."

Paulette's jaw dropped open. "Wait a minute. You're not saying—"

Mike raised his free hand and massaged his rugged jaw. "A little here, a little there. Filling in the face, that is. Worked wonders. Maybe you ought to try it."

Paulette huffed, but Carrie just bit into her bottom lip and raised her eyebrows.

"And the gym helped too, of course," Mike continued, finding himself getting more and more carried away. "But I said to myself, I said, nothing's too good for my Carrie. She wants a certain type of man, she's going to get it…"

Carrie held her breath and watched Paulette's eyes widened.

"I mean, why not?" Mike asked. "You women do it all the time, reinvent yourselves for your men. Breast augmentation—"

Paulette went positively white and glanced down at her own flat chest.

"Come on, Wilson," Carrie said, nudging him soundly with her elbow. "Time you talked to a few more of our guests…"

"And not," she whispered sternly in his ear, when they'd left the mortified Paulette behind them, "about breast implants." In spite of her admonition, Carrie found herself fighting the urge to giggle. From the time she'd been fourteen, Carrie's first cousin Paulette had made it her personal goal to steal every man in Carrie's life right out from under her. Well, not this time, Carrie thought, glowing brightly as the man on her arm looked down into her eyes with a naughty grin.

"She deserved it," he whispered back. "Not only did she suspect the truth, she was coming on to me besides."

Carrie looked back over her shoulder at Paulette, who was downing a fast cup from the punch bowl, then broke into a chuckle. "Oh Mike," she said, patting his arm. "You're absolutely right. Busybody Paulette got just what she deserved. But do you think she'll tell?"

Mike looked straight over the top of Carrie's head. "I think she's leaving. Hope she wasn't your maid of honor or anything important like that."

Carrie spun around to see the back-porch door swinging shut at Paulette's back. "Holy cow!" Carrie exclaimed, stretching up on her toes and giving Mike's cheek a firm peck. "How on earth did you do that? I've been trying to get Paulette to keep her nose completely out of my business for nearly twenty years and never even came close to succeeding until now."

Mike's cheek tingled where Carrie's warm lips left their mark, reminding him ever-so-pleasantly of the type of fiancé he was expected to be. Touchy-feely. Amen, Mike thought, winding his arm around Carrie's shoulders like a prayer. She was truly radiant today. Looking very bride-like in her white linen dress, its clean lines unintentionally outlining every curve. Even its scooped neckline, which professed its innocence by camouflaging itself with a hint of lace, looked positively villainous in its enviable position right next to Carrie's bosom.

"What? What is it?" Carrie asked, bringing a hand to shield her briefest hint of cleavage. "There something wrong with my dress?"

Mike gave her shoulders a reassuring squeeze and planted a light nibble on her tantalizing neck. "Nope, nothing at all. I was just thinking about how great you look in white."

Carrie slapped a palm into the side of Mike's head. "Behave yourself! Grandma Russell's coming!"

"Just playing the part," Mike said, drawing her into an affectionate hug and kissing her lightly at her temple. "Of the loving fiancé."

Carrie blinked as her world went cold and hot. Hot and cold. No, wait! Her palms were sweating, but her belly was a pit of ice.

"Carrie, darling!" An elderly lady with more salt than pepper in her short curly hair scuttled over and wrapped frail arms around the two of them.

"Wilson," she proclaimed, beaming up at Mike and whacking him soundly on the shoulder. "I do declare, you *are* a hunk!"

Somewhere in the heat of the moment, Carrie found her tongue. Which was, dammit, stuck to the roof of her mouth.

"Grandmother!" Mike exclaimed, lifting the 110-pound woman into the air with his bear-hug embrace. "It's so good to finally meet you."

Well, now, Carrie thought, Mike was carrying things a little far. Paulette was one thing, but...

Mike set Grandma Russell down as she reached up and pinched his cheek. "He is a doll, Carrie! An absolute doll! Just somehow I never pictured him as a blond. You should have told me he looked like Robert Redford but green-eyed, young, and sexy."

Mike laughed out loud but felt his ears tinge hot just the same. Though he was used to compliments from women, up until now, most of those offering their rabid appreciation had been under fifty.

"Come on, darling," Grandma Russell said to Mike. "Let me show you off..." She gave a little chuckle. "Show you around, that is. Carrie's aunties are all dying to meet you."

Carrie swirled the ladle nervously around the near-empty punch bowl. The shower had gone off without a hitch. She and Mike—uh, Wilson—had even gotten some lovely gifts. A blender, cooking utensils. Towels. All the nice little odds and ends that help make a newlywed house a home. This wasn't such a good idea, after all. In fact, it was terrible. So many people had gone to so much time, trouble, and expense. Even Nellie's place cards were beautiful. A keepsake for the happy couple. Carrie frowned at her murky reflection centered in the twirling ice ring.

And to make matters worse, Mike had been an absolute champ. Everybody adored him implicitly. He'd been warm, witty, and charming the whole afternoon through. His act as her fiancé had almost even seemed real; at least his hugs and affectionate glances had seemed authentic enough. And those few unexpected kisses, though innocent enough in their placement—one at her temple, one on the back of her hand, the one at her neckline… Well, all right, maybe the one at her neck hadn't seemed quite so innocent in intent as the others. But still, no matter where his kisses had landed, each time Mike had surprised her with the warm contact of his lips, her world had caved in and her heart had let go. Let go of any notion that this thing between them was little more than make-believe. Because, though words could deceive, feelings seldom lied, and when Mike brought his flesh to hers… Carrie dropped the ladle into the punch bowl as goose bumps tore down her spine.

Carrie felt the hair swept from her nape. "Ready to leave?" Mike whispered, bringing his mouth close to her ear.

Carrie turned in surprise and found herself directly in his arms, her backside pinned against the table that held the punch bowl. "Never," she said, bringing her arms up and around his neck and pulling him in close as their lips melded in the final consummation of what they'd both been desiring all afternoon.

"Why don't you kids run on home?" Grandma Russell asked, blinking the dining room chandelier on and off above them.

Mike pulled back in a damp sweat. "Let's!" he said, giving Carrie a firm, virgin peck on the lips.

Carrie sat in Mike's car, anxiously fiddling with his radio and waiting for his return from the grocery store. Though he'd said he'd only be a minute, she could only guess at what he'd buy. Champagne? Wine and roses? Were things between them really moving that fast?

And where on earth would they go? She wasn't sure she was ready for Mike to see her place. Besides, she was totally unprepared for company, and her cottage was a total wreck. Though the setting, at the western edge of the county, was gorgeous, the inside of her home looked like it had been hit by a black tornado. If there was one thing Carrie didn't do well, it was clean. Well, in truth, her laundry skills weren't so hot either. All the whites always seemed to come out a weird shade of neon pink. Even after all this time, Carrie couldn't figure out which of her red sweater tops had been doing all that running.

The driver's door popped open, startling Carrie from her reverie.

"Miss me?" Mike asked with an earnest grin.

"Absolutely," Carrie said, hoping her face didn't look nearly as hot as it felt. "What you got there in the bag?"

"Uh-uh," Mike said, scrunching the paper roll at the top of the bag a bit tighter and slipping it into the backseat. "It's a surprise."

The only problem was, Mike still hadn't settled on the perfect place to share it. Not at his place, for sure. His apartment was a pigsty. Not that it was usually that bad... Mike slumped back against his bucket seat at the inner half-truth. The fact was, compared to its usual state, his apartment looked good. Which wasn't saying a whole heck of a lot.

Mike could tell from meeting her family and seeing the tidy home she'd grown up in that, though she hadn't been raised rich, she'd definitely inherited class and style. A style that would be severely undone by the sight of his dirty boxers strewn all across the backs of his chairs. And those beers cans... Mike scratched the back of his head, trying to remember if he'd put that last batch of trash out to recycle. Better not chance it, he decided, heading the car west of the city.

"Where to?" Carrie asked, a fine sweep of color caressing her cheeks, but only half as tenderly as Mike wanted to at this moment.

"Someplace special," he said, lowering his window just a crack to let in a refreshing breath of cool evening air.

But deep inside, Carrie knew that it scarcely mattered. Someplace special seemed to be right here with him.

****

Chapter Nine

Mike hoisted Carrie down from the top of the split-rail fence and led her into the vineyard.

"Well, what do you think?" he asked, clutching his mystery paper bag to his chest.

Carrie inhaled deeply, absorbing the scent of summer hills and lilac. For acres before them, rows upon rows of trellised vines bloomed in lush splendor, their endless trails spilling toward the tumbling Blue Ridge. Mountain upon haze-tipped mountain fell backward in smoky array, blending infinitely with the settling twilight.

"It's gorgeous, just gorgeous," Carrie said, talking not only of the scenery around them. For in this afternoon alone, she'd seen something altogether different in Mike. Not the tempting bachelor, nor the friend with a penchant for making her smile. But a regular family man. Carrie was certain now he hadn't been fabricating his desires for that white picket fence. Mike was good in a crowd, great with people—young and old alike. And playful to boot. Carrie was sure he'd make an excellent father.

"Care to sit?"

Carrie looked down, realizing Mike had removed his jacket and laid it as a cushion on the ground for her to protect her clothing.

"You know," she said, taking a seat and arranging her dress on the jacket to defend it from the spreading clay-dotted grass around them. "Alexia was really a very stupid woman."

Mike grinned in surprise and scooted in beside her on the splotchy earth. "Kind of you to say so."

"I mean it," Carrie assured him. "But she was smart in one regard."

Mike raised his brow in expectation.

"Picking you out in the first place."

Mike sputtered a laugh. "Alexia always was a good shopper."

Carrie tried to keep her eyes focused ahead of her, but it was impossible not to be drawn to the man beside her. Never in her life—nowhere in the world—had Carrie St. John come across the likes of Mike Davis. He was handsome and charming, absolutely. But much more importantly, he was genuine.

"You know the thing about Alexia—"

Carrie reached out and latched on to his rugged chin. "Mike."

He stopped midsentence and questioned with his eyes. Beautiful, earth-moving, sea-green eyes.

Carrie settled her other hand at the side of his face. "Shut up and kiss me."

"Thought you'd never ask," he hummed, closing in.

After they'd necked like teenagers for nearly twenty minutes, Carrie felt something moist and clammy seeping onto her outer thigh.

"Oh my God!" Mike said, looking down in horror at the leaking paper bag pressed up against Carrie's leg. "Your beautiful dress!"

Carrie puzzled at the mysterious green stain on her leg. She wiped a hand against the sticky mess, then brought a palm to her nose. "Mint?"

"Mint chocolate chip," Mike said, sheepishly unrolling the bag. "Ice cream sandwiches."

Carrie threw back her head with a belly laugh. "Ice cream sandwiches! And there I thought you'd gotten us another elegant vintage of wine."

"Carrie," he said, pulling a clean handkerchief from his pocket and dabbing the side of her clothing. "I'm so sorry about your dress. I forgot all about—"

"That's all right," she said, giving his chin an affectionate nuzzle. "I did too. And no worries. The dress will wash." And if it didn't, she could always get another. But Carrie was as certain it wouldn't be so easy to replace Mike Davis. "Think they're still any good?"

"Of course! A little soggy, maybe," he said, pulling the soppy package from its dripping bag. "But edible, nonetheless. How about it?"

"I'd love one." Carrie smiled. "Mint chocolate is my absolute favorite. How on earth did you know?"

"Wild guess," Mike said, grinning naughtily. "And your Grandma Russell told me."

"Cheater!" Carrie said, swatting him playfully across the chest. "You just wait till I corner some of those old high school chums of yours and get the dirt on you!"

"So, you're not disappointed, then?"

Carrie warned herself to proceed with caution. "In…?"

"The ice cream. I mean, it may not be the rare vintage you were—"

"I love the ice cream. I don't think any man has surprised me with ice cream before." Much less spread it on my thigh, she heard herself thinking but thank God didn't say. All of a sudden, Carrie was developing lots of innovative ideas about what she and Mike could do with ice cream. But not here, not now, not in the middle of somebody else's vineyard.

"What is this place?" Carrie asked, taking a bite out of her dripping sandwich and delighting in its fresh minty taste. Nightfall was almost upon them, shadows stretching long over the vineyard. The top third of the mountains had already faded to black. If they didn't head back soon, they might have difficulty finding the car in the darkness.

"Just a place I stumbled on long ago."

"It's yours?" Carrie asked, surprise and delight firing her eyes. "I should have known you were a vintner! Now, it all makes perfect—"

"Carrie," Mike answered, crestfallen. "It's not mine." He couldn't bring himself to tell her that he'd only worked here as a hired hand during his high school summers. That his background was much more modest that hers ever was. He and his dad never had a nice home—of any size—to call their own. They had rented and lived out of trailers. His graduation from Ashton had been thanks to a full athletic scholarship.

"Maybe you should buy it, then?" she continued, seeming happily excited by the notion. "It would make a wonderful investment!"

"Investment?" Mike had never been able to invest in anything beyond his next month's rent.

Carrie appeared to pick up on his mood and halted. "Oh, I'm sorry," she said, wadding up her ice cream sandwich wrapper and balling it in her fist. "It wasn't my place at all to suggest that."

And why, indeed, would she suggest it? Just as breezily as if wishing could make it so. Did Carrie St. John actually have that sort of money herself? "Would you invest in it, Carrie?" Mike pressed, wanting to know if his hunch was accurate.

Criminy. Carrie had really painted herself into a corner this time. Here she'd been all this time not wanting to let on she had money, and then she went and said a stupid, unthinking thing like that. "Why, no. No." Carrie felt herself growing warm in the chill of the evening. "Just making conversation, that's all," she lied, scrambling to her feet. "You know, it's getting late…"

"I know," Mike said, looking deep in her eyes as if trying to discern something.

"Think you could drive me back to the inn so I can collect my car and get on home? I have to work tomorrow and I'm sure—"

"No problem," Mike said, scooping their litter off the ground and trying to discern what she was hiding. Mike weighed the dichotomy of her simple, small-town roots against the exceedingly preferential treatment Carrie had been afforded by Charles Gilpatrick back at the inn. Was Carrie St. John filthy rich, someone famous to be reckoned with?

"Who are you, Carrie St. John?" Mike asked as the breath of night threaded silken silence between them.

"Just a simple old girl from Virginia," she said, needing him desperately to believe it.

****

Chapter Ten

Carrie made the forty-five minute drive from the country inn to her country bungalow with her top down. The nippy evening air lit up her senses and helped her focus her attention on the issues at hand, as weaving wind whipped fingers through her long, loose hair. At least she'd had her wits about her when Mike had dropped her back at the parking area and had been able to concoct that missing earring story that had allowed her to duck back inside. She'd watched out the window of the inn until a few minutes after Mike had driven away. Though here he'd been insistent about staying and seeing her to her car, she'd fabricated an excuse about also having to settle some business arrangements with Mr. Gilpatrick that might take a while.

While in looking at his watch, he'd seemed dubious, Mike had finally acquiesced and settled for a formal good-bye on the steps of the inn. The same stone steps where Carrie had first beheld him in his dripping-wet, near-naked glory on that fated night they'd met.

Carrie's throat went dry at the recollection as she sailed through the yellow light. Carrie quickly checked her rearview mirror, but saw, with relief, that even the cops in this sleepy berg were already in bed tonight. Carrie felt the spreading heat at her collarbone and inhaled deeply, fighting off the thought of anything that put Mike Davis and beds together in her mind. She was falling for him. Falling badly. And there didn't appear to be a darn thing she could do about it except for trying to keep this silly illusion from blowing up smack in her face.

How long did Carrie really believe she could go on like this? A week, a month? In the outstanding event their relationship endured beyond Mike's reunion, sooner or later he was bound to start asking questions. Already had started asking questions, Carrie reminded herself.

Criminy.

Carrie ran a hand along the back of her stiff neck as she wheeled her car onto the exit ramp that led to the isolated country route that would take her home.

Oh what a tangled web we weave...

Carrie slowly shook her head.

All she'd really wanted was for Mike to like her for herself. But now she wondered precisely what that was. A liar? A manipulator? Someone with just as little integrity as Mike's old fiancée Alexia?

Carrie blinked hard as hot tears pressed with biting force from her bleary eyes. It was no wonder she'd never found a man. There, without even trying, she'd gone and done it again. Screwed her love life all to heck and back. Love life, ha! she thought, laughing bitterly into the wind. As if she'd ever truly known the meaning of the phrase.

Mike scurried around his apartment, tossing empty aluminum cans into the recycle bin. Holy cow! He didn't know why he had so much nervous energy. But whatever the reason, he might as well put it to good use.

Mike paused in the threshold to his bedroom, mentally trying to calculate when he'd last changed the sheets. Well, if he couldn't remember, then the likelihood was they needed changing again.

Mike tugged back the fitted sheet, trying to recall the last time he'd actually had a woman in the place. Alexia, neatnik that she was, had always insisted he come to hers. Alexia had always insisted on a lot of things, like her pleasure first, for example. Not that Mike minded giving a woman pleasure. That aspect, in fact, excited him. But when it was that woman's pleasure to the exclusion of everything else in the world, including the presence of her partner...

Mike shook his head and carried the pile of sheets to the washer. He was quite certain Carrie wouldn't be like that. Carrie was a warm and sensuous woman. Inviting yet giving all at once. It was there in the way she kissed, the way she teased and beckoned with her eyes. The way her tantalizingly womanly curves ached for a masculine touch...all...over...her body...

Christ.

Mike looked down at his boxers, realizing he was going to need another cold shower. His second since he'd dropped Carrie off at the inn and come home. And, for crying out loud, their parting kiss had been nothing if not chaste.

Maybe that was what it was. She was driving him to distraction by holding back. Though, when he was being honest, Mike had to admit that Carrie wasn't the only one who seemed adept at putting the brakes on their relationship. While their mutual attraction was too strong to deny, there was something else holding each of them back. Mike couldn't put his finger on it exactly. But his gut told him it had to do with more than just the faux-fiancé game going on between them.

Mike heaved a heavy sigh and flipped on the cold water. What was it about Carrie St. John that always left him all wet?

Carrie rolled over in bed and lazily lifted her cell. "Hello?"

"A dillar, a dollar..."

"Grandma Russell?" Carrie asked, her head pounding. She squinted against the bright light streaming in through the tilted Venetian blinds.

"Lands sakes, child, did I wake you? I thought you investment types were up catching worms well before dawn!"

Carrie reached out her free hand and angled her clock radio toward her so she could read the time. Ten thirty. She'd missed her nine-thirty appointment. Carrie's head fell back against her pillow with a thunk.

"No, Grandma." She held aside the receiver and yawned. "Been up for hours."

"Well, sweetheart, you're not really sounding too chipper."

"Just a stress headache," Carrie said, massaging her throbbing temple. "It will get better." Already, Carrie was making a mental list of all the conference calls she'd have to rearrange. Mondays! What a mess!

She must have been exhausted. Totally wiped out from her weekend experiences. And it was all Mike Davis's fault.

"Well, maybe my cheery bit of news will leave you feeling better... That fiancé of yours—"

Carrie sat bolt upright in bed, not knowing quite what to expect.

"—is such a doll. You'll never believe what that Wilson did!"

"No, I probably wouldn't," Carrie said, meaning it absolutely.

"He sent the sweetest note—with the flowers."

"Flowers?"

"Yes, indeed, perfectly gorgeous arrangement. Must have cost the man a fortune, but, of course, like you've told us, the man is dirty rich, so it really is the thought that counts."

Carrie's temples constricted and pounded anew. "Filthy, Grandma. The term is fil—"

"Well, now, sweetie, you may call the man a dirty rascal if you want to for outfoxing you with this sweet surprise, but I wouldn't go as far as to insult his personal hygiene. In fact, he looked exceptionally well-groomed to me!"

Carrie's head thumped back against the headboard, ramrodding the base of her skull with another lightning bolt of pain. Flowers? He'd sent flowers? How in the world would she ever explain breaking off an engagement to a wonderfully thoughtful man like him now! Her grandmother was totally smitten! "It was a very sweet gesture, but I'd caution you against taking anything he said too much to heart."

"To heart?" Grandmother Russell shot back. "The man has a heart the size of Nebraska! Looking forward to being a part of your beautiful family was what he said. Brought tears to Nellie's eyes it did. Real tears, not just the ones she sometimes puts on during confession."

Carrie sighed and squeezed shut her eyes, wondering how on earth she was going to get out of this mess, while her grandmother continued to wax poetic on "Wilson's" attributes.

"Wasn't that just the most eloquent…"

Carrie could practically feel the steam blowing out of her ears. Nice job, Mike Davis! Playing the perfect gentleman and leaving poor Carrie holding the bag. The time for beating herself up over her own duplicity had ended. Now Mike was the one with the answering to do. And Carrie was going to see to it personally he did some talking.

Mike was just going out to get his mail when Carrie roared into his apartment's parking lot like a storm cloud on the wings of—holy cow—a new-model BMW convertible. She did have money. And lots of it.

That wasn't the only thing, Mike saw, backing up a step as she leapt from her car and made for him like a thunderbolt. "You!"

Mike inched back toward the mailbox. He'd never seen a woman so positively incensed. Not even any of the several who'd dumped him.

"Hi, Carrie," he offered lamely, as she walked right up to his chin, then poked him in the chest.

"Thanks…one…whole…heck…of a…lot!" she said, emphasizing each word with the pressure of her pointy finger. "You, Mike Davis, have single-handedly ruined my existence!"

"Hey, whoa…" He tried to lay a steadying hand on her shoulder but backed off when the look in her eye told him she just might bite it off.

"What right," she asked, again with the pointy finger that—dammit—was starting to hurt, "do you have…sending flowers…to my grandmother?"

Mike gripped his hand around the offending digit and held it in place.

"Let me go!" Carrie charged.

"Only if you promise to stop poking."

Carrie glared at him and pulled back her hand, massaging its aching joints. Poking into his chest had been painful for her as well, though she didn't dare let him know it. It had taken her over three hours to find him. She'd gone through six other Michael Davises in Redfields before she'd finally happened upon this place here. And now he owed her some answers.

"Like some iced tea?" Mike asked, pinned to the mailbox, his eyes darting furiously between Carrie's still-idling car and the woman in front of him.

Carrie ran a frustrated hand through her tangled hair. "Well, for heaven's sake," she said, her shoulders sagging just a tad so their positioning didn't look quite so combative. "I'm not a bee that's going to sting you."

"Tea?" Mike repeated, his voice coming out an octave higher than intended. Okay, Mike, he told himself, now would be a good time to think up the reason you did that. She obviously wants an explanation. But do you understand it first?

All he knew was that when he'd awakened that morning feeling sunny, sending flowers seemed the perfect thing to do. Gracious. Thoughtful. And the truth was, he adored Carrie's grandmother—along with the rest of her extended family.

Carrie set a hand on her hip and shook her head. "All right, I'll come in for tea, but under one condition. You promise to be completely honest with me."

"That cuts two ways, Carrie," Mike called as she walked back to her car and yanked her keys from the ignition.

Criminy. She hadn't even considered that.

Carrie sat across from Mike at his kitchen table in his tiny but tidy efficiency apartment. Carrie looked around, somehow finding all the cleanliness disheartening. More undeniable proof of just how highly unsuited to each other the two of them were. What had she been thinking?

"Well," Carrie asked, setting down her glass. "I'm waiting."

Mike was waiting too. Waiting for something brilliant to occur to him. But all he could come up with was the very embarrassing truth: he'd wanted to impress Carrie's family.

"It wasn't meant in malice, Carrie," he began tentatively, pushing aside his tea glass.

"Well, of course, I know that!"

"Well, then…?" he asked, gently pacing his words, lest her iced-tea glass wind up on his head. "Why are you so darned mad?"

"I'm mad because… Because…" Carrie faltered. She was so furious she could barely form her words. But what, in truth, drove her anger was even beyond her comprehension. All she knew was it had something to do with Mike inserting himself deeper in her life than he had a right to go.

"We made a deal, you and I."

"That was ages ago."

"Three days," she corrected without blinking.

"Well, it seems like ages, Carrie. It seems impossible I've only known you that long. The two of us, we…"

"What?" she demanded, looking him square in the eye.

"You can't tell me you don't feel it too?"

Carrie pushed back from the table and stood. "No way. No way, Mike, are you turning the tables back on me. We are not here to discuss my feelings!"

"Okay," Mike said, taking a lingering sip of tea. "Shall we discuss mine, then?"

Panic gripped Carrie by the throat. What was happening here? No! She was here to confront him. She was furious! And there he was looking—what? Humble? Self-effacing? Forgivable?

Carrie bit into her bottom lip and dropped back down into her chair. "What do you mean by that?"

"What I mean," he said, looking right through her with earnest green eyes, "is that you said you wanted honesty. I'm prepared to fess up, if you are."

Carrie gulped and grabbed her tea glass, which was empty.

"Refill?" she asked weakly.

"In a moment," he said, reaching across the table and encircling the hand that gripped her glass with both of his. "First, we talk flowers."

Carrie tried to steady her resolve, remind herself of just how infuriated she was. But when she looked at him, really looked at him, Carrie knew in her heart Mike was telling the truth. He hadn't sent those flowers to upset her. Or anybody else, for that matter.

"So why?" she asked, the still air settling around them as Mike released his grip on her hands and laid his palms on the table.

"I can't tell you what it felt like. Being there in that room of people—with your family. I felt so included. Really a part of things. I didn't mean to make anything harder on you. Truly, I didn't. I just wanted to say thank you."

The gratitude part she could buy. He seemed sincere enough in his emotion, but… "The note?"

Mike wrinkled up his brow. "Guess I crossed the line on that one. My apologies. I sometimes get so swept up in things, I act before I think."

Carrie held her tongue, knowing very much what that felt like. Okay, so maybe he had acted on impulse. And maybe out of good intention. But what a viper she was going to look like now when she announced her relationship with Mike had ended.

"How about your family?" she asked after a long pause. "Don't they make you feel—included?"

Mike gave a slow, sad smile and studied the tabletop. "Well, I guess family's a pretty subjective word, isn't it? Mine isn't all that big, really. Just me and my dad."

"Oh, I'm sorry." But Mike didn't offer any more. He just sat there being very quiet. Abnormally quiet.

Carrie studied the man with the gorgeous green eyes and shoulders broad enough to take on anybody's troubles. It wasn't only his trick with the flowers that was going to make ending this charade difficult.

After what seemed like eons, Carrie reached across the table and laid a hand on his arm. "Mike?"

"My dad's sick, Carrie," Mike said, looking up with moisture-tinged eyes. "Very sick. For the past two years, almost all of my income has gone to his care."

Carrie felt the raw burn in her throat. She'd never known her parents. They'd died in a house fire when she'd been barely a year old. By a twist of fate, she'd been staying with her grandmother as her parents were planning on going away together for their second anniversary trip. They'd never made it, and Carrie, thanks to the luck of the draw, had survived to be raised by her Grandmother Russell and doting great-aunts.

Still, she couldn't imagine what it would feel like to lose someone who'd looked after you, somebody you'd equally loved and cared for. Carrie bit back the sting in her own eyes, realizing her Grandma Russell's time probably wasn't that far away.

"I'm so sorry," she said. "I had no idea."

"Well," Mike said with a shaky smile, "Dad's had a good life. A good hard life, lived the way he wanted to live. I can't fault him for that."

"What's he got?"

"It's more like what hasn't he got? His liver's going, he's got heart trouble. But, you know, the great thing is he's still out there kicking. Tough old coot..." Mike's voice faltered. "My dad. Still got that great sense of humor. In fact, just to look at him, you'd never..."

"Oh, Mike." Carrie stood from the table and walked to where he sat, putting her arms around him. Her heart went out to this man. This man who always tried to put on a good face, who had worked so hard to make her laugh... Who had sent her grandmother flowers. Who could kiss like nobody she'd ever known.

"Now, don't go feeling sorry for me," Mike cautioned, looking up and returning her hug.

"What I feel for you," Carrie said, for the first time admitting it to herself, "goes way beyond sorry..."

Oh great, Mike thought, she pities me. That's even worse.

"And the love I see in your eyes for your father only reconfirms it. I've seen somebody very different here today. And yesterday, at the shower also. It's not just that you're a warm, caring person. Not just that you can make me laugh..." Not just that he looked like sin, she told herself.

Mike drank her in with his eyes, beholding a million new possibilities. Then stood to cradle her in his arms.

She was going out on a limb here, and she knew it. But the words that were welling within her were so fierce, so true, she was losing all power to hold them back.

"Mike, I think that I'm falling in love."

Mike nestled her closer and brought his forehead to hers, kissing her sweetly on the lips. "Only think?" he asked with a twinkle in his eye.

"Oh Mike." She brought soft hands to his cheeks and looked at him deeply. "More than think. I know it's brazen of me to say so. That it will probably take a while for you to feel the same way. I don't understand what has happened to me. How all of this has happened so fast. I never really thought…"

Mike hushed her by tracing the tender line of her lips with one finger. "You don't know how long I've waited to hear you say that."

"But Mike!" she said, splaying her hands against his chest. "We've only known each other three days."

But three minutes was all it had taken for Mike to know. The moment he'd seen her holding court at the top of those stairs at the inn, Mike had ached inside at the feeling someone like her could never be his. And now, every ounce of his being ached at the possibility that she could.

Mike couldn't believe that any woman as warm, as wonderful, as completely genuine as Carrie, could be standing here professing her love. But she was. And not just with her words—with her eyes. Eyes that searched his soul and begged answers to so many questions.

"Carrie," he said, kissing her at first lightly and then feverishly before pulling back. "I want to make love to you. With you. For as long as you can possibly stand."

Carrie grinned as the smallest—daintiest—tingle took hold of her tailbone, then spread like rapid fire. "That's the best offer I've had all day," she said with a kiss.

****

Chapter Eleven

Mike took Carrie's hand and led her back into the sparsely lit bedroom. At the height of the afternoon, it was unmistakably the brightest room Carrie had ever had occasion to make love in. She'd always required it dark and comfortable. For her, that was, and her multitude of figure flaws. But here, in the light of day, with nothing but Mike's king-size bed before them, there was nowhere to hide.

Carrie thought of asking Mike to close the blinds but then saw the single shade was already drawn.

"Come here," Mike said, pulling her down onto the bed beside him. "Let me look at you."

She was as beautiful as ever, a patterned sarong skirt wrapping around her curvaceous hips. Her knit sweater top highlighted every curve.

"I think," Mike said, reaching up to touch her face as they lay sideways on the bed, "that I've died and gone to heaven."

"You're not dead yet," she assured him with a kiss.

"Then why do I feel like I'm floating?" he asked, running a stroking hand up and down her bare arm.

Carrie's skin ignited at his touch as his caress wandered lower, strumming over her hip, wending around to her bottom, where he gave her tush a playful squeeze.

Carrie colored in spite of herself.

"You're not inexperienced, are you?" Mike asked, bringing his nose to hers and nesting a hand in her hair.

"Heavens no," she said, coloring again. And feeling all the while like a liar. She'd never experienced anything quite like him. Her heart was beating so furiously she was certain it would break free from her chest cavity at any moment and make a mess of the bed.

But Mike assured her with his heated kiss they'd find others ways to dirty the linens entirely.

"I knew from the moment I saw you," Mike said, rolling her onto her back and straddling her legs with his own, "that something would develop between us."

"You knew this?" Carrie asked doubtfully, tugging lightly at his derriere and situating him comfortably on top of her. Boy, he felt like heaven. All six foot two of manly heaven. And, positioned just right.

"Well, I hoped it actually. You looked so pretty standing there. So defenseless—"

"Defenseless?" she challenged, lifting her head from the pillow.

Mike chuckled and kissed her sweetly. "No, my love…"

Carrie's heart fluttered at the sound of that.

"You are absolutely right. You are many, many things, but defenseless is not among them."

"Mike," Carrie said, wrapping her arms around his shoulders, "it's getting hot in here."

"Baby," he replied, bringing his mouth to hers. "You don't know the half of it."

With that, he clambered off her, taking her elastic-waist skirt along with him in one swift, tugging motion.

Carrie brought her hands self-consciously to her outer thighs, but Mike reached out and held her wrists captive.

"You, Carrie St. John, are the most exquisite woman I've ever seen. Please, don't hide from me."

With that, he released his grasp and gripped the hem of her knitted top, yanking it deftly up and over her head in one smooth move. Carrie willed herself not to dwell on his apparent ease at clothing removal but to focus instead on the calming lull of his eyes. Eyes that seemed to be looking down and into her. Steadying, reassuring that nothing—and no one—else on this earth mattered.

"Carrie," Mike said, bringing his lips to her cleavage, just above her bra, his hands cupping both breasts. "You're beautiful."

Carrie sighed, leaning back against the mattress, sure she must be dreaming. Savoring the sensation of his touch as she reached out and explored the leanness of his hips, the tautness of his derriere.

Carrie felt for his belt buckle and unhitched his pants as he kissed her with the desperation of a dry man in the desert seeking water.

"Carrie," he said, cradling her head in the muted light of the room. "I've waited a lifetime for you."

Though all reason argued against it, her heart dared to believe as she reached for his shorts and slid them down toward his knees.

Mike briefly righted himself and did away with his clothing. All of it.

Carrie marveled at his size, at his rigidity, longing to make him all hers.

"Here," she said, pushing down her panties and urging him to help her.

He stripped away those and the last barrier of her bra with skilled ease.

"Mike, don't you think—"

But he was already miles ahead of her and unrolling a condom onto his ready form.

And Carrie was ready too. Oh so ready, like she'd never been in her lifetime.

Mike reached up and gently gripped her breasts in his hands, then rocked slowly onto her, carefully aligning their bodies until their lips and every other inch of them met exactly where they were meant to.

"Ready?" he asked, sliding his hands up her rib cage, alongside her shoulders, up her neckline and into her hair.

"As ready as I'll ever be."

"Then I," Mike assured her, filling her slowly, single-mindedly, with his manly need. "Am going to show you just what loving is…"

He gave her a tender smile. "Until you cry uncle," he said, bringing the furnace of his mouth down on her own.

"Uncle!" Carrie cried, several hours later.

Mike raised a moist chin from between her legs.

"Uncle, uncle, uncle!" she yelped, slapping him on the shoulder. "My God, are you trying to kill me?"

Mike grinned and fell down on the mattress beside her. "Just trying to take you to heaven, angel."

"Been there and back. There and back. And then some," she assured him breathlessly, tugging at his arms.

"Good, then that means you liked it?" Mike asked, sweetly stroking her knees. The sensation of his touch—lingering, strong, tender—sent shivers racing to her core.

"Liked it?" Carrie exclaimed, raising herself up on her elbows. "Gracious. Now that I've, uh, tasted it, I fear I'll never be able to live without it!"

Mike fell down on the mattress beside her and pulled her tightly into his arms. "Precisely what I wanted to hear."

"I've really got to go," Carrie said, trying halfheartedly to escape once again.

Mike linked his arms around her naked torso and nibbled the small of her back. "Uh-huh."

"Don't you have a job?" Carrie asked in exhaustion. Already it was Tuesday. Heaven only knew where the past eighteen hours had gone.

All Carrie knew was that she was hungry—and late for work.

"Probably not anymore," Mike answered. "But real estate was never really my calling anyhow."

"No," Carrie said, turning on the bed and kissing the man behind her fully on the lips. "Your talents run much deeper than that."

Mike hooted and sprang from the bed. "I've got it! How about we go to breakfast!"

"Breakfast?" Carrie asked, sitting up and clutching the comforter to her chest. "But I have to get to work! I never even reported in yesterday."

"Great," Mike said, coming around the bed and kissing her on the top of her head. "Then you've set a precedent."

Carrie's eyes traveled the nude expanse of his body, thinking over all the precedents the two of them had set within the last several hours. There was no denying it. Mike Davis had positively swept her away. "Well, I suppose I could phone my secretary…"

Mike shot her a triumphant grin. "Get showered," he said, striding to the bathroom and returning with a towel, which he lobbed in her direction. "I'll make the coffee."

"Like that?" Carrie asked, observing his stunning form.

"What's a matter?" he teased, "too sexy for you?"

"Goodness, no," she answered. "Just sexy enough. Just don't count on getting to breakfast anytime soon," she said with a growl as she leapt from the bed and tackled him to the carpet.

Mike bit into his bagel with gusto. Apparently, he'd been just as starved as she was. "You know, Carrie," he said between mouthfuls, "I don't think this reunion thing is going to be very hard to pull off."

Carrie laughed affectionately and ran a tender hand down his face. "No," she answered, "I think we've got that touchy-feely part down pretty well."

In between their hours of lovemaking, they'd also done some soul-spilling. Among other things, they'd both revealed how much each one had been itching to get physically close to the other. Carrie had confessed that the whole "touchy-feely" pose regarding Wilson had been a total sham, and Mike had admitted how he'd eagerly planned to take advantage of that idea.

Well, she supposed they both were satisfied now. Carrie blushed at the thought as the waiter refilled her coffee.

They were in a small diner a few miles from the hometown university. The place, it turned out, where both Carrie and Mike had secured their undergraduate degrees and Carrie had later gone on to graduate school in pursuit of her MBA.

Mike still didn't know about the money. And Carrie still wasn't sure if she was willing to tell him. There she was, a hopeless, helpless mess. Totally in love with a man she'd known for less than a week but who'd seemed in tune with her soul for a lifetime. Could she really risk messing it all up now? They hadn't even made it past the hurdle of the reunion and her hidden mission of impressing his friends.

Not to mention the very pointed fact that, in spite of all of his words of love, despite the way he looked at her and made her feel, Mike still hadn't said *"I love you."*

"Penny for your thoughts," Mike said, clinking his coffee cup to hers. "Feeling tired this morning?"

Carrie lifted her coffee cup to her lips and smiled naughtily over its rim. "Not as tired as I could be."

Mike laughed in surprise. "Why, Carrie St. John," he returned with a sly wink. "You are insatiable."

Only with you, she replied in her heart. Only with you.

"Okay, here's the plan," Mike informed her as he stood kissing her good-bye at her car. "First of all, you and I phone in to be sure we still have our jobs."

Carrie laughed and mussed his hair. Tuesday had somehow melted into Wednesday, and then Thursday had come along straight out of nowhere. In between it all, they'd gone out to restaurants, called in to their respective offices occasionally with "no show" excuses, and done plenty of dirtying of Mike's sheets.

"You probably ought to do the laundry while I'm gone," she teased with a poke at his chest that had now become a silent joke between them. At one point during their hours of lovemaking, Mike had maintained she'd merely given him her rigid finger as a phallic encouragement. Carrie swore to herself with a grin, she'd never give anyone but Mike Davis that sort of finger again.

"Hey, baby," he said, leaning in close and nibbling her neck. "You trying to tell me something with that finger…?"

"Mike!" she said, swatting him on the backside. "You don't watch yourself, the two of us will not only be out of jobs, we'll entirely miss your reunion."

"And what a tragedy that would be," he said, enfolding her in his arms.

"Okay," she said, reaching behind her and popping open the driver's door. "I'm going this time. Really, really going."

Mike raised one sexy eyebrow. "Well, personally, I like it better—"

"Don't you even say it, you beast!" she said, climbing into her car. "Heavens, I've become involved with an animal."

"Aw, come on now, Carrie," he said, leaning in over her door, "you know you love it."

The truth was she did. But for now, she decided, the satisfaction of that knowledge would be hers and hers alone.

****

Chapter Twelve

Carrie unfolded the tissue and heartily blew her nose. "Oh, Grandma Russell," she sobbed. "It's no use. There isn't going to be any wedding!" She'd decided it was time. Time to tell the truth about the whole sordid affair. Now that she'd fallen in love with Mike, she couldn't have her grandmother go on thinking he was Wilson. And—with Wilson out of the picture—there was that little matter of a wedding to cancel. Something that she'd been putting off and putting off, and finding excuses not to do.

"Now, now, honey," her grandmother said, reassuringly patting her hand. "Don't go blowing things all out of proportion like you sometimes do. I swear, you must get that from your Aunt Nellie."

Grandma Russell leaned forward and lifted her china teacup off the low tabletop in front of them. "Drink your chamomile, dear. It will make you feel better."

Carrie wrung her tissue in exasperation. Her grandmother apparently hadn't heard a word she'd said. She'd come here first to confess and secondly to beg moral support. Possibly even to seek approval—and forgiveness—for her new choice. But all she'd received thus far had been tea and crumpets with some prattle on pre-wedding-day jitters.

"You don't understand," Carrie sniffed. "Tonight's the big night."

"The reunion. Very sweet." Grandma Russell smiled as if in fond remembrance. "Dear Wilson told us all about it. He was so very proud at the prospect of having you on his arm. Never knew that New York man of yours had such local roots." She shrugged with a thoughtful smile. "Well, I suppose that does explain the accent."

Carrie set down her teacup and rummaged through her purse for her aspirin.

"If you ask me," her grandmother offered, unsolicited, "you keep popping those things, you're gonna get a hole in your stomach."

Carrie ignored that bit of advice and downed two tablets with her, by now, room-temperature tea. "It's not just the reunion, Grandmother. It's looking serious. He's taking me to meet his father!"

"Wonderful!" Grandma Russell said, clapping her hands together. She paused a moment, looking puzzled. "Are you saying you've not yet met him? And what do you mean by serious. Of course it's serious. You're getting married, aren't you?"

"No," Carrie said, dropping her eyes to the sofa and wishing with all her might she could sink right between its cushions. "No, Grandmother, I'm so sorry. There isn't going to be any wedding."

Grandma Russell set her cup down so firmly on its saucer the two pieces rattled. "Nonsense, Carrie girl! That's just pre—"

"Grandma," Carrie said, looking up through streaming eyes. "No. I'm sorry. Really, really sorry I waited until now to tell you. But I…"

Her lower lip began a violent tremble that prevented her from finishing.

Grandma Russell turned sideways and swept her into her arms. "There, there, child. Everything's going to be all right. I promise it will. Nothing at all that Wilson could have done could merit all this. There is always a way—"

"He left me, Grandmother," Carrie said, finally finding her voice. "Just like that. No warning at all. And," she said, her voice taking on a renewed tremble. "For another woman."

Grandma Russell stiffened in shock. "That letch! I never in a million years would have believed that charming man capable of—"

"Not that charming man," Carrie corrected with a shake of her head. "Wilson."

Grandma Russell's ebony eyes went wide as saucers. "Wilson? What are you saying, child? That the man you brought home—"

"An imposter," Carrie admitted, hanging her head.

Grandma Russell straightened her spine. "Well, he looked real enough to me."

"No," Carrie said, forcing herself to press ahead. "It was all a ruse. We met at the Sawyers House."

"That local inn you financed?"

Carrie nodded and kept going, lest she lose her nerve. "It was really kind of funny, in fact. When I met Mike—his name is Mike, by the way."

"Good, solid, masculine name," Grandma Russell interjected.

Carrie gave her grandmother a twisted smile. No matter what the rest of Carrie's story, Grandma Russell had quite obviously made up her mind.

"Mike Davis. Guess you like the Davis part too?"

Grandma Russell smiled warmly. "It does have a certain ring to it. Listen, sweetheart, you can fill me in on the particulars you'd like to. But it really isn't necessary. Like the television commercials say, life happens.

"So Wilson was a creep and left you. Good riddance to that one, I say! And this Mike—Mike Davis, the man who not only can't keep his eyes off you in a crowded room but also wowed your family, just happened to be at the right place at the right time. I think it's beautiful. It's fate. And he's a hunk. You're three for three on this one. Looks, tenderness, compassion… What on earth are you staring at, child? Did I forget to wax my mustache?"

"Do you really think so?" Carrie asked, studying her grandmother's face for wisdom. "Believe Mike and I met for a reason? That in spite of our odd beginnings, it was somehow meant to be?"

"Certainly, I think so! Didn't I ever tell you how your grandpa and I met?"

Carrie shook her head. She'd thought she'd heard all of Grandma Russell's stories by now, but this, apparently, was a new one.

"It was back in the days of panty raids…" her Grandma began sheepishly.

Carrie chortled. "They still do those, Grandmother."

"Do they now? Well, how prehistoric! At any rate, as I was saying, it was back… Well, whatever! I'll just cut to the chase and tell you. The October of my Freshman year at the Women's College, there was a panty raid on my dorm one night. And your old grandpa just happened to be below my window in the marauding crowd."

"You threw your panties at Grandpa?" Carrie gasped. From the little she remembered of her grandfather, he'd always seemed such a straight arrow.

"Not my panties, heavens no. Needed those. Tossed something much more enticing…"

Carrie waited patiently as her grandmother drew out the moment for suspense.

"Myself!"

"Yourself? You threw yourself out the window?"

"Well, not intentionally or anything like that. But I was young, you see. A brand-new student. And it was all so exciting and hedonistic. The very idea of panty raids."

Carrie giggled, trying to envision her white-haired grandparents in the picture Grandma Russell was painting.

"Well, anyhow," her grandmother continued. "I was leaning out the window just a bit, trying to get a better look at the boys down below. One was quite handsome. Tall, redheaded, sure of himself. Looked to me like a Scot."

"Grandpa," Carrie guessed.

Grandma Russell smiled, then chuckled at the faraway memory. "Indeed, it was your grandfather. And a very striking young man, at that. Well, I happened to catch his eye, you see. I could tell because there he was at the bottom of the window looking straight up at me. Not chanting or carrying on like the other boys. Just very stoically standing there, looking up with the most curious smile. And then it happened. Somebody moved behind me, and I lost my balance and fell. Tumbled right out the window and over the sill—straight into your grandfather's arms!"

"He caught you?" Carrie gasped.

"More or less." Grandma Russell grinned and turned a curious shade of plum Carrie didn't think she'd ever seen on her grandmother. "But the important thing is, even the parts he didn't catch survived the fall. It was only half a story, with the back of our building constructed into a hill. But still, from that time on, your old grandfather and I had a lot of fun joking about that fateful day I 'fell' for him."

Carrie studied her grandmother, trying to discern whether what she'd just shared was honest-to-goodness family lore or a simple cock-and-bull story. Either way, Carrie knew and appreciated exactly what her grandmother was trying to do.

"So, then," Carrie said, balling up her tissue and tucking it into her purse. "There's something to this fate business after all."

"Not a doubt in the world."

Carrie's face fell. "But we'll still have to cancel the wedding, Grandmother. I've been avoiding making all the calls. Every time I've picked up that telephone, something inside just wouldn't let me do it."

"Well." Her grandmother smiled. "Maybe that something inside knows there is going to be a wedding after all."

Mike stared into his closet and frowned. Less than two hours to showtime and not a thing to wear.

He scratched his head, thumbing through the several designer suits Alexia had given him. It was no wonder he didn't like his wardrobe. It was all a patent reminder of not-so-pleasant times gone by. Well, all right, maybe not all of it.

Mike pulled out a charcoal gray suit, one of the few he had purchased on his own. The others, he realized, would have to go. Not to mention that glaring ring on his dresser.

Why Mike had waited so long to return Alexia's ring, he really couldn't say. For sure, he needed the money. And the Caymans...

Mike laid out his suit on the bed, recalling the long, lazy, and often playful afternoons most recently spent with Carrie. Was chasing his dive-shop dream really all it was cracked up to be? If that was still what he so desperately wanted, why hadn't he already cashed in that ring—or called the jewelers, at least, to make arrangements.

Mike walked to the mirror hanging above his dresser, realizing the startling truth. There were simply far too many things holding him to Virginia. His dad, of course, was currently on his own. But eventually, he'd need more personal looking after. Mike had already done some investigating. Private-care arrangements were expensive.

No way could Mike realistically budget for those and still be able to sink money into starting a new business.

And then there was Carrie to think of. Carrie St. John, the woman who'd admitted with a full heart that she loved him and whom his own raging insides told him he loved back. And yet Mike hadn't been able to find the words to tell her. Perhaps because he was still coming to terms with the concept himself. Or maybe, more critically, because he believed on a superstitious level that, by admitting his feelings, he would somehow jinx what was happening between them.

In spite of his track record, Mike had never told any woman he loved her. Not even, surprisingly, Alexia. Adore, yes. Worship, on occasion. But love? Those three little words had never slipped from his mouth. And the reason for this was crystal clear, Mike saw, looking in the mirror.

The day he finally uttered those words would be the day he was prepared to ask a woman to be his wife—and really mean it. None of this marriage of convenience BS or racing to beat any sort of artificial time clock. Just a true, honest desire to share the here and now, and forever after, with the woman of his dreams.

Mike's eyes dropped to Alexia's ring, glistening on the dresser top. Maybe returning it wasn't what he needed to do after all. Perhaps that was what the hesitancy in his gut about taking back the ring had been trying to tell him all along.

Mike walked to his nightstand and picked up the telephone to call the jewelers—with one very important question.

Carrie reached behind her and zipped the back of her red-sequined dress. She straightened and studied her reflection in the mirror, hoping she wasn't going overboard.

The plunging neckline, though not untasteful, still might be a little much.

Carrie held a couple of dangling earrings up to her lobes and considered the picture. A little too uptown? Licentious, even? The lady in red...

Carrie walked to her closet on her tiptoes, carefully lifting the hem of her dress off the polished oak floor. With heels on, the length was perfect. And the height difference between her and Mike certainly allowed for any size heel Carrie desired.

With Wilson standing five foot ten, only two inches above her own five eight, she'd always had to be more careful.

Carrie stopped considering the two pairs of shoes in her hands and realized for the first time she hadn't thought of Wilson in days. Of course, she'd mentioned him in her conversation with her grandmother. But, in truth, even in speaking his name then, she'd thought more of his imitator Mike than Wilson himself. In fact, it appeared Wilson had been replaced entirely by Mike Davis.

Oh dear. Carrie made her shoe choice, then gripped her hem and tiptoed back over to the bed, wondering if this was good. She'd warned herself sternly about the rebound thing. But surely this wasn't what this was. It was fate, a preordained opportunity—just like Grandma Russell had said. And if she ever thought of Wilson Haywood again, she conceded, it would have to be in gratitude. For had he not dumped her on precisely that day at precisely that time, she wouldn't have wandered down to that pool.

Carrie sighed, recalling her startling introduction to her "swim god." Not nearly as dramatic as what had happened to her grandmother but certainly unforgettable in its own special way. Carrie would never forget how Mike had taken her breath away when he rose from the water, dripping wet, insinuating moisture racing down every trail of his muscular body.

Carrie swallowed and sat to slip on her shoes. Well, maybe the dress was a little showy. But she'd clearly seen enough of Mike that he deserved reciprocation.

Carrie blushed at the notion that he found her beautiful. That he found her body enticing, alluring…feminine. Not only had he failed to mention her "figure flaws," he, in his manly appreciation, appeared totally unaware they existed.

Carrie slid in the earrings, then stood to examine the total effect. The dress was exquisite, the shoes and jewelry the perfect complement. But what shone out among it all was the light in her eyes. The fresh color in her cheeks. The first dewdrops of love everlasting.

If Mike could do this to her now, Carrie realized, she'd be a real stunner by the time she reached Grandma Russell's age.

****

Chapter Thirteen

Mike took the winding country road that snaked through the open tract of undeveloped land. As per Carrie's instructions, he started counting mailboxes when he got to the top of the hill. When he hit number four, he made a hard right and steered down the gravel drive that led through a covering of trees. And then his passage through the cluster of woods spilled out into open pasture. A huge purple-blue sky draped with lazy clouds danced high above the nearby mountains. The scenery took his breath away.

Mike spotted the small white-stucco house nestled back against the edge of the property. And, as he drew closer, he spied its immaculate gardens forming a meticulous border around the cottage's outside. Boxwoods and azaleas, tastefully interspersed by wild flowers, lavender, and zinnias. And nearer the railing of the small wraparound porch, towering sunflowers strained skyward to catch their last glimpse of the fading day.

Up on the porch there was a swing, patently built for two. Mike sighed, taking in the idyllic picture, thinking the only thing that would make it complete would be a passel of kids playing in the grassy yard that butted up against the neighboring orchard.

Mike suddenly looked down at his watch, realizing he'd been sitting there daydreaming. Daydreaming about a home and a houseful of kids. His kids, he realized with vibrant shock. His and Carrie's.

Mike scrambled from the car, warning himself to take things slow. Follow through with his premeditated plan. For all of his previous slipups, this was one thing he was going to get right.

Mike stepped up onto the porch, straightened his tie, then rang the doorbell. When nothing sounded inside, he tried waiting a few moments, then knocking instead.

A few seconds later, Carrie pulled back the door. "Oh, I'm sorry, did you try knocking? I've been meaning—"

But Mike stopped her with a deep, rumbling, "Wow! Carrie, you look like a million bucks."

Another point she'd made plans to discuss with him, Carrie reminded herself, making space for him to scoot by her into the room. "Thanks, you look terrific too." And, boy, did he ever. Very stylish in his charcoal gray with muted pinstripes.

Carrie shut the door behind them and looked down at her dress. "You sure this isn't too much for tonight? I mean, I didn't really know how formal the dinner-dance was going to be."

"You look perfect," he assured her, a panther-like look in his eyes. "Absolutely perfect. In fact," he said, pulling her into his arms, "if I hadn't already promised you dinner…"

"Mike!" she protested, pushing back on his shoulders, "you'll muss my hair!"

"That won't be all," he said, kissing her sweetly but then pulling back when she exploded in laughter.

"Have my skills deteriorated that badly?" he asked, offended.

"Oh no," she said, laughing as she reached for a tissue from the entrance table and dabbed his lips. "It's just that you're wearing my Magenta Rose." She chuckled again. "And, I'm not so sure that's the impression you wanted to give at this reunion."

"Ah," Mike said, smiling and kissing the tissue in understanding. "Better now?"

"Don't know." Carrie brought a hand to her chin. "Maybe we ought to try it again, just to be sure?"

Mike gave her a teasing wink. "Why, Carrie St. John, if you keep threatening me with kisses…"

"No, no," she said, lifting her purse off the table. "You promised your dad we'd be there at six and it's already half past. If we're going to have any opportunity for a visit before the dance, we'd best get going."

"Only if you promise we can play that little lipstick game later on."

"All you want," she said, beaming up at him as he held back the door.

Mike pulled open the screen door of the trailer, letting Carrie inside.

Jack Davis stood from his chair at the kitchen table with a cat-calling whistle.

"Dad!" Mike admonished, standing beside Carrie just inside the door.

Carrie's cheeks lit with color, but she remained composed as she crossed the small room and extended a warm hand in the older man's direction. "Mr. Davis—"

"Nope," he broke in, taking her hand and surprising her by pulling her into a bear hug. "You, young lady, can call me Jack."

Carrie returned his firm squeeze.

"Jack," she said, patting his back. "Mighty glad to meet you."

Jack pulled back and gave her a broad, welcoming grin. "She's even prettier than you let on, boy," he directed at his son. "Might just think about keeping this one for myself."

Mike walked over and whisked Carrie out of his
father's arms. "Sorry about that, old man. But I got to her
first, and you know what they say—"

"Finders, keepers," Mike and Carrie parroted together.

Jack's eyes sparkled. "Quite a handsome pair the two
of you make. So, when's the big day?"

Mike swallowed hard.

"June 23rd," Carrie raced in. "The church has been
reserved for months."

Jack shot Mike a quizzical look. "That so? I was under
the impression the two of you had only recently met."

"Yeah, but I'd been hoping," Carrie said, giving Mike
a megawatt smile.

June 23rd? What on earth…? Oh, okay, Mike got it.
Maybe this was all a little part of the rehearsal for Carrie's
big performance at the reunion. Well, fine, he could play
along with that. For now. Assuming Carrie accepted his
authentic proposal—and that was still a big "if," his dad
certainly wouldn't mind a change in dates later on. Jack
wasn't, and never had been, a stickler for details.

"It's a really long story," Mike said, reaching down
and taking Carrie's hand. "The important thing is, we've
already set some of those…uh, wheels in motion."

Mike didn't know the half of it, Carrie thought, giving
his hand a squeeze. Not only did they have a church and a
reception hall reserved but also a caterer and a three-
hundred-dollar wedding cake. Mint chocolate, through a
little creative rearranging, on Carrie's part, she thought,
feeling rather proud of herself. The only thing standing in
their way was the minor detail of the formal marriage
proposal. And that little nuance of Mike's admitting he
loved her, which, by now, she was quite certain he did.
He'd brought her home to meet his father, hadn't he? Even
Alexia, as it turned out, hadn't gotten that far.

"Yes," Carrie said, taking the chair at the table Jack had offered. Mike pulled out another and sat beside her. "But we can get to all those details later. We still have plenty of time."

Jack shook his head with an eye on his wall calendar. "Looks more like two weeks, by my calculation. Now I don't know much about women stuff, planning weddings and all that, but it really seems to me the two of you might be cutting things a bit tight here."

Carrie and Mike looked at each other.

"Not that I'd want to do anything to discourage ya!" Jack said, whacking Mike across the shoulder in a sign of approval. "You just tell me what I'll need to do from my end."

"Not a thing, Dad. Not a thing."

"You could walk me down the aisle," Carrie raced in impetuously. She bit her lip in hesitation as Mike dropped his jaw and stared. "I mean," she continued tentatively, "I never knew my father, and Grandpa's been gone for years…"

"I'd be honored," Jack said, a barely perceptible moisture gathering in the corner of one eye.

Holy cow! Was she nuts! How could she even do this to him? Why would she even do this do him? Nothing like this was in his presupposed plan. Though he'd hoped to ask that big, big question. He was still smack dab in the middle of finessing the hows and whens. Now, if he didn't act soon, he'd be lunch meat in his father's eyes. Just look at him! Less than ten minutes flat, and his dad was already eating right out of Carrie's hand!

"Uh, Carrie, sweetheart," Mike said, laying a hand on her forearm resting on the table. "Don't you think that invitation is a little—premature?"

"Premature? Heavens no!" she said, wriggling her arm out from under his grasp and glowing at Jack. "Like your dad said, our wedding is only two weeks away."

Our wedding. It was the first time Mike had actually heard her say it. And it sent simultaneous shivers of delight and terror straight through him. This was really going to happen. He and Carrie. All pretending aside. Holy cow.

Mike withdrew a hanky from his breast pocket and dabbed his dampened brow.

"I agree," Jack said. "Two weeks is no time at all. Besides," he said, looking very pointedly at Mike, "she asked me, not you, young man. So, stay out of it!"

Jack returned his affectionate gaze to Carrie. Though his hair had gone completely gray, Carrie could definitely see where Mike had gotten the gorgeous green eyes from. "So, young lady, tell me a bit about yourself. You from these parts?"

"Yes, sir, grew up in Mill Creek, right around the bend. And Mike and I, as it turns out, both went to the university."

"Not together, I would guess? You seem a good bit younger than Mike."

Carrie grinned. "Only a few years, sir. But, you're right, we're far enough apart that we weren't in school at the same time."

"Ships passing in the night," Jack commented with a rather melancholy smile.

"More like swimmers," Mike mumbled under his breath.

"What's that?" Jack asked when Carrie burst out laughing.

"He's just being silly," Carrie said, kicking Mike under the table.

"Won't be the first time," Jack said. "Well, at least it's good to see his taste in women has improved. Are you working in the area?" he asked Carrie.

"Yes, I'm an investor."

Jack whistled. "Big money in that, hear tell."

"Dad…" Mike cautioned in a low vibrato.

Not here, not now, Carrie told herself. "Uh, yes, sir. Yes, sir, there is."

Carrie glanced down at her styled gold watch, the one she reserved just for evening wear. "Oh my gosh, will you look at that! Seven fifteen. How far a drive did you say it was?" she asked, turning to Mike.

"Hey, yeah, we'd better get going," he said, standing from his chair. "Dad," he said, giving his father's shoulder a pat. "You take care, now. And no more flirting with those nurses. If I get one more call from Dr. Shafer's office about your hitting on the staff…"

Carrie laughed all the way to the car.

"Does your dad really hit on the nurses?" Carrie asked once she'd adjusted her seat belt.

"Only the pretty ones."

Carrie smiled and shook her head as Mike started the ignition. "Now I definitely see where you get it from." But what Carrie secretly found herself wondering was if any of her and Mike's children would be half as bad.

****

Chapter Fourteen

The parade of oaks leading up to Ashton Hall was magnificent. Though Carrie had heard of the all-boys boarding school, she'd never once been there. Likely because the high school circles she'd run with didn't exactly involve a "moneyed" crowd.

Carrie had plans to discuss her financial "predicament," meaning the fact that she was exceedingly wealthy, with Mike tonight. The time for pretense was over. He'd proven well enough, in a million different ways, that the woman he cared for had nothing to do with her bank account. Of course, he'd seen her car and knew she worked in finance. What he didn't know was that her title in New York was Venture Capitalist and that her account balance registered in the seven digits.

Carrie prayed inwardly that it wouldn't make too much difference. Mike certainly didn't strike her as the sort of man who would feel emasculated by a wife who made more money. The impression he'd given her was that Alexia had been well-off, and that, in and of itself, apparently hadn't fazed him in the least. "Thank you for doing this," Mike said, shutting off the engine and pulling his keys from the ignition. "You don't know what it means to me to have you on my arm tonight."

Oh yes, she did. Because whether or not he suspected it, it meant just as much to her. And not simply because she planned to pose as his fiancée for the night. But, more importantly, because she hoped to soon make that role a legitimate position.

Mike walked around the car and opened her door. "You ready to be my bride-to-be?" he asked with a grin that sent her stomach all aflutter.

More than he knew. But she just said, "Yes."

Ashton Hall was an impressive two-hundred-year-old red-brick building, elegant, high white columns flanking the tall main entrance. The striking Georgian architecture reminded Carrie of parts of the college campus where she and Mike had both studied.

"Wow," Carrie said as Mike ushered her in the door.

The domed central ceiling, in and of itself, must have reached over forty feet. Elegant crystal chandeliers dripped light like sparkling teardrops onto the well-placed circular tables that dotted the perimeter of the room.

White linen tablecloths lapped hand-sewn oriental carpets. And above the clatter of clinking glasses and conversation, a band played jazzy eighties tunes from a stage set up far against a back wall.

The mood was all genteel opulence. They'd been standing there scarcely five seconds when a server strode briskly over, offering up a tray of champagne.

"Carrie?" Mike asked, lifting a single flute off the tray and extending it in her direction.

From the trailer park to this. All at once, the disparity hit her. "Thank you," Carrie said, accepting the champagne.

Mike picked up a glass of his own, and the white-gloved server made himself scarce.

Carrie took another look around the room. "I said it before, but it bears repeating. Wow."

"I know it must seem odd," Mike said. "I mean, after seeing the place I grew up."

Carrie heated at the notion that he'd read her thoughts. How embarrassing. He probably assumed her to be judging him. "No, actually—"

"It's all right. Really. Though I may have been somewhat ashamed of my humble roots as a teenager..."

"You should never have felt ashamed of your father, Mike. He's a wonderful man."

"Easy for me to accept now," he told her as they made their way into the busy room. "Not so easy for a boy in high school. I landed at Ashton Academy like a total fish out of water."

"Scholarship?" Carrie guessed.

"Swimming."

She might have known. "Well, I think it's fantastic you had the opportunity. When I was a teenager, I didn't even know places like this existed."

An attractive couple wandered over. A pretty blonde and a stocky brunet about Mike's age. The husky fellow set his glass on a nearby table and took up Mike's free hand with great gusto. "Mike the Spike!" he said, cheerily pumping Mike's arm. "Great to see you, buddy!"

Mike's eyes lit up. "Figaro? Oh, my... How are you?" he asked with unfeigned delight. "Uh, oh, forgive me. Carrie St. John, this is Fig."

"Fig's not his real name," the blonde interjected. "It's Paul. Paul Westinghouse III."

Mike chuckled and turned his eyes on the woman. "Why, hello. Are you the lucky missus?"

"Am at that." She smiled. "My name's Wendy. And you, officially, are...?"

"Mike Davis," Carrie supplied, easily following the protocol where the women spoke for the men. She could get used to that. "But I want to know where that 'spike' part came from," she said, playfully poking Mike in the chest.

Mike looked down at her rigid finger and chuckled at their private joke. "Now, don't go getting any dirty ideas," he whispered in her ear. He turned and winked at Paul. "Spike comes from the way I used to dive."

"Straight out like this," Paul said, striking a pose by extending his arms arrow-straight over his head. The group broke out laughing.

"And Fig?" Carrie asked with a grin. "I can't fathom that one."

"That's because he swam like a song," Wendy reported. "You know, *Figaro, Figaro, Figaro*..."

"Yeah, a swan's song," Mike chimed in.

More companionable laughter.

"So, you two were on the swim team together?" Carrie asked.

"Yes, ma'am," Paul answered, "though it looks like your husband's keeping much more fit than I am. Congratulations, by the way," he said, turning to Mike and once more pumping his hand. "Somebody made an honest man of you after all."

"Well, not quite," Mike began.

"Yeah," Carrie said. "He's still as dishonest as they come."

Paul and Wendy roared.

"Know what you mean," Wendy added. "Once incorrigible, always incorrigible. Wedding band or no."

Wait a minute! What was happening here? He was assumed to be married? Mike shifted and dug his left hand into his pocket.

"Well, buddy," Paul said, lifting his glass in Mike and Carrie's direction. "Guess you had us all fooled. Heartiest congratulations on your excellent taste."

When Paul and Wendy had made their polite good-byes and departed to mill with other guests, Mike turned to Carrie. "Holy cow, those guys thought we were married!"

"Imagine that," Carrie said with a curious poker face. "Well," she said after a brief silence, "stop staring. It's what you wanted, isn't it? To be known as the man who beat his perpetual bachelor status?"

"Well, yes, but—"

"Look," Carrie interrupted. "People are getting seated. We'd better find our places before they start serving."

Mike and Carrie were lucky enough to find their place cards at the same table with Paul and Wendy and a few more of Mike's old swim-team cronies. Mike looked around the room, seeing that many of the other groups that hung together in high school had also been placed together at their respective tables. Whoever had been in charge of the seating chart had done an excellent job.

The various courses flowed by with good conversation and wine, both of which seemed in endless supply. Everyone at their table was duly impressed with Carrie, both her financial acumen and her personal style. Mike could tell by the body postures of his former fellow athletes who seemed intent on angling close to Carrie to absorb her every informed word on the financial markets. Either that or to catch a whiff of her heather perfume, which made Mike more than just a little bit jealous. Though he didn't know why. She was doing exactly as he'd hoped she would, knocking the socks off every one of his buddies. If only they didn't look like they'd be happy to also have Carrie knock their boxers off...

"You've been quiet," Carrie whispered in his ear. "Getting tired?"

"Just tired of the conversation," Mike whispered back.

"Ah," she replied, her tone still hushed, "finance bores you."

"No," Mike said, his voice coming out louder than intended. "Men putting the moves on my 'wife' bore me."

The two couples seated across the table from them stopped conversing and stared.

Oh Jesus. Mike pushed back his chair and stood. "Excuse me, I'm going to get some air."

"Then I'm coming with you!" Carrie said, scrambling to her feet and hurrying after him.

Carrie followed Mike out a large glass door that led to a sweeping veranda, then settled beside him on a carved marble bench. She couldn't believe it. He was jealous! All rationale told her that was a bad sign. The books, the magazines all told you that jealousy meant possessiveness. But way deep inside, Carrie's heart was doing a jig, shouting *yes, yes, yes!*

He loved her; she knew he did. All she had to do was get him to say it.

"If any of those men were flirting," Carrie lied, "I certainly didn't know it."

"Flirting? Carrie, Billy Smith looked like he was ready to up and carry you away! That, with his wife Elizabeth sitting next to him!"

"Mike," Carrie said, scooting in toward him. "Only one man in this crowd could carry me away. And I think you know exactly who that is."

Oh, if only, Mike thought, looking up at the big, bold moon. But what if when he really asked, she said no? Mike had nothing to offer her. Nothing but what was in his heart. And Carrie already had it all. He knew from talking to her grandmother. Feeling it only right, he'd gone by this afternoon to discuss his intentions. Grandma Russell had assured him that the money business didn't really matter one way or another. And, at the time, feeling hopeful, he'd believed it.

Now he just didn't know. Mike had seen the way Carrie's jaw had dropped when she'd walked in here. Though she came from more humble roots like he had, this was the sort of world she was meant for. That ambition was what had taken her to New York. And to see the way she had meshed with his Wall Street buddies at the table, he guessed that was where she belonged. Certainly not stuck permanently in Central Virginia with the likes of him, much less down in the far-off Caymans. Mike heaved a sigh, his heart heavy with the moment.

"Penny for your thoughts?" she said, lightly touching his arm.

"Carrie," he began, "there are some things I need to tell you."

"No," she said, laying a hand on his thigh. "Me first."

Mike looked up into her beautiful dark eyes sparkling with starlight.

"I think," she began, then stopped. *Come on, Carrie, don't lose your nerve.* But what if he couldn't love her for who she really was, a woman with money? What if he said they were too different, that their lives were worlds apart?

"What do you think?"

"Mike, I have something personal to tell you. I mean, personal about my job. Of course, normally, it's nobody's business, so I don't discuss it at all. But with a man I… What I meant to say was… Criminy!"

"Criminy?" Mike asked, leaning in and raising her chin.

"Oh gosh, it's an expression I picked up from my grandmother."

"Speaking of your Grandma Russell…"

"No, Mike," she said, lightly brushing aside his hand. "Let me finish. It's very important to me I get this out—before I lose my nerve."

Mike set his palms on his thighs and waited.

"Mike, I'm—"

"Dirty rich," he said, turning his eyes on hers.

Carrie gasped. "Have you been talking to my grandmother?"

"Carrie, beautiful Carrie," he said, cupping his hands over her satiny shoulders. "Did you for one minute think that wealth would be a hindrance?"

Carrie nodded but saw nothing besides her own confusion mirrored in his eyes.

"Honey, the only one setting up roadblocks here with his miserable life is me. You, Carrie St. John, have everything any woman could ask for. You're intelligent, attractive, accomplished at your job—and rich. I, on the other hand—"

"Oh," she said, scooting back and out of his grip. "So you are holding my bank account against me."

"That's not what I said."

"Well, it's certainly what you implied by telling me I already had it all. For your 411, I don't. At least not what I most want in here." She stopped and thumped her chest. "And in case you haven't heard, money can't buy you love."

"Oh, I know that for certain," Mike assured her. "And for your information, though I had suspicions you had money, my falling in love with you had nothing to do with your bank account!"

"Your what?" she asked, her voice softening in disbelief.

Holy cow! He'd gone and done it. And for crying out loud, right smack in the middle of the closest thing they'd had to an argument yet.

Carrie reached up and pinned his face between her hands. "Repeat what you just said."

Do it better this time, Mike warned himself. Much better.

"I, uh…" Mike swallowed hard past the lump in his throat. "Carrie, it's true. I know I was a jackass at dinner…" Oh great, he was doing just wonderfully. Curse words and all. "I mean, I know I overreacted. But, in truth, it drove me crazy seeing those other guys vying for your attention. And it made me think about… Realize just what a danger it would be to have you on the open market." Nice, Mike. Real smooth, you unromantic doofus! Well, at least she wasn't laughing.

It was all Carrie could do to stifle a chuckle. He was trying so hard it almost hurt her to watch. For all his experience with women, it was overwhelmingly obvious Mike Davis was, at this moment, mapping uncharted territory.

"Carrie St. John," he said, the words erupting from his throat like red-hot lava. "I love you."

Carrie wasn't sure whether he looked more amorous or petrified, but whatever it was, she understood that Mike had just put his heart on the line.

"And I love you back," she said, bringing the cushion of her mouth up to his.

"Now," she said after their long, languorous kiss, "let's go dance while the two of us still seem to be agreeing on something."

"I don't like to dance," Mike protested.

"Oh yes, you do," Carrie answered with a mysterious grin. "I'll prove it."

Carrie was right about the dancing part, Mike thought, reveling in the comfort of her curvaceous body snuggled up against his own. The song playing was a band arrangement of Led Zeppelin's "Stairway to Heaven." It had been the only song in high school, Mike recalled, shutting his eyes, that even the nerdiest guys could get a dance for. Though he wasn't prepared to tell Carrie just yet, in his day, the swim-team fellows weren't the most sought after of the jocks. Mike's early successes with women came later, in college. But now, thinking back to his Ashton days and gently swaying to the music with Carrie, he was glad for every forgotten dance. Every pigtailed, pug-nosed girl who'd ever rejected him. And yes, even snooty Alexia. For if it hadn't been for any of them, he would have had no way of knowing exactly what he held in his arms now.

The music slowed to a stall and polite applause, and Mike feared the band leader would pick up his tempo. But instead he sent a smile over Carrie's shoulder and gave Mike a knowing wink as he began a slow, jazzy rendition of "Lady in Red."

Carrie didn't know if the music was still playing, or if it was merely the pulse of her heart that was lending rhythm to her feet. All she knew was that she felt protected, sheltered, and loved. Wholly and unconditionally drawn straight into Mike's warmth. They couldn't have been more connected had they been in bed together. Or maybe they were, and she was dreaming.

Mike reached up and stroked her hair, causing her to melt into him another inch. He'd never peel her off now. Carrie couldn't even say where Mike ended and she began. The only thing she knew for certain was that she never wanted this feeling to stop.

"I'm sorry, folks," the band leader said, lightly tapping Mike's shoulder. "But we're closing up."

Carrie opened her eyes in astonishment to find the room had cleared. Only a few staff persons remained, busily bussing tables and stacking up chairs.

"Holy cow," Mike said, squinting into the brightness of the lights that were now turned way, way up.

"Holy cow is right," Carrie said, bolting back into foggy reality and sweeping a hand through her hair. "We've shut the place down!"

****

Chapter Fifteen

A few hours later, Carrie stroked a hand down Mike's naked chest and snuggled deeper into the crook of his arm. "You know," she said as moonlight threaded through the spreading oak outside and danced with the sheers at the open window, "I really loved being your wife tonight."

Mike tightened his arm around her and kissed the top of her head. "And I really loved the honeymoon," he said with a growl.

"Mike!" she said, swatting his biceps.

Her hand relaxed against his skin and began to massage. He was all solid muscle but with just enough give. Rock hard, with a covering of bristly masculinity. Carrie shivered as she felt a renewed stirring in her loins. It was true. She was insatiable with Mike. But then what woman in her right mind wouldn't be? No woman who would ever get the chance to find out again, Carrie told herself securely.

"You know," Mike said, trailing a finger down her back to the point where it met the sheet. "You were right about that dancing part. I sound like a sappy movie, but I could have danced all night."

"Hmm," Carrie said, laying a light kiss on his shoulder. "But I'm awfully glad we came back to tango here."

Mike chuckled and patted her backside. "I could get used to this."

Carrie's heart stilled.

"Carrie?" Mike asked, as the wind rattled the window panes. "How would you feel about making things more permanent?"

Carrie's insides did cartwheels, but somehow she'd gone mute.

"I mean, I'm not asking—yet."

"What?" she asked, finding her voice.

"You'll have to trust me on this. I really want things to be perfect. You deserve perfect."

Carrie didn't understand. Nor could she imagine anything more perfect than this. "This—"

Mike rolled sideways and shushed her with a kiss. "You'll have to trust me, okay? Just swear you won't go running off with any of my old swim-team buddies within the next couple of days."

"Not a chance," Carrie said, her heart thundering as he threaded his fingers in her hair and brought his mouth to hers.

"So?" Grandma Russell asked. "Tell all, sweetness! Details, details! You haven't been answering the phone all morning."

Carrie walked to the kitchen with her portable phone and poured her coffee. "I'm answering now, aren't I?"

"Yes. But that only proves he's finally gone."

Carrie smiled into her coffee mug, feeling wicked. For some reason, Grandma Russell's accurate suspicion that Mike had stayed over didn't embarrass her. She was a grown woman, after all. And her grandmother, for one, didn't sound the least bit offended. "Why, Grandma Russell!" Carrie said, feigning shock.

"Goodness, child," her grandmother retorted, "I wasn't born yesterday. So, tell me. I'm all ears. Did he pop the question?"

Carrie frowned. "No."

"No?" her grandmother said with surprise. "Well, that's a man for you. Probably waiting till the time is right."

Now it was Carrie's turn to be surprised. "Grandma Russell, you are one cagey old bird, aren't you? How ever did you know?"

"Tweet, tweet," her grandma said with a chuckle. "Oh darling, just because my hair's gone mostly gray doesn't mean I've forgotten entirely how the male species operates. You can chase them back all you'd like during the courting stage, but when it comes to asking the 'big one,' most men still want to feel like it's their idea. Even if it generally isn't."

Carrie took a sip of her coffee and sat in the big easy chair that afforded her a view of the mountains. "Men!" she said, but her mood was lighthearted. He'd said he loved her. Loved her! And then that talk about making things permanent.

"Indeed," Grandma Russell answered. "But who, honestly, wants to live without them?"

Carrie knew that she didn't, not any longer than she possibly had to.

"So," her grandma asked. "We still on for the 23rd? The caterer phoned this morning, wanting the second half of her money."

Carrie hesitated. Talk about risky investments… But now was not the time to push Mike with a timetable. Her grandmother was right. At this point, it was important for him to take things on his own terms. To go at his own pace. Carrie thumped the table nervously with her free hand. "Sure," she said, biting into her bottom lip. "Why not? It's only money."

Grandma Russell laughed. "You, child, are probably the only person I know who could say that and really mean it."

Mike got down on one knee and looked up at his father. "Okay, Dad, tell me how this sounds…"

"What you got your elbows all sticking out for? You trying to imitate a chicken?"

Mike pursed his lips and stood. "Are you going to cooperate or aren't you? I thought you liked her."

"Love her, son. She's a regular doll. And, not so incidentally, probably way too good for you. But I can't for the life of me understand what you're all so hellfire worried over. You never practiced up for any of the others."

Mike blew a hard breath and ran his fingers through his hair. "Well, maybe the other times weren't nearly as important."

His dad laughed and shook his head. "You, boy, are the only man I know who asks women to marry him just as easily as most ask girls out for burgers."

"You aiming to insult me?" Mike asked, setting his hands on his hips.

"Nope. Just wondering. Does Carrie know about the long line of others before her?"

"She knows about Alexia."

"And what about Marianne? The one with the big…" Jack made a curvy motion in the air with his hands.

"You really do have a one-track mind, you know that?

Jack twisted his lips in scrutiny. "You're really going to do it this time, aren't you? What about that island thing? You always said if you found the right girl to share your dream…"

Mike felt the sweat form at his brow. "Carrie doesn't even know about that island thing. Besides," he said, unable to keep his face from falling just a bit, "like you're so fond of saying, Dad, you can't have it all. At least, not if you come from the same side of the tracks we do."

Jack raised his eyebrows and studied his son. "If you'll recall, boy, another thing that I'm fond of saying is, it never hurts to ask. Have you even talked with her about it?"

"Ridiculous," Mike said, shaking his head. "The whole notion is pie-in-the-sky at this point. Besides, if she says yes to my proposal, I'm going to have to find a way to up my income here. Not go tossing pennies in a far-off well. I've been thinking that maybe I could talk my broker, Colleen, into making me a partner. My sales have been really high lately, after all."

"I thought Carrie was well-off."

"Exceptionally well-off. Precisely why I can't let her think I won't carry my weight. Maybe it's old-fashioned of me, but I inherited my values from you."

His dad gave him a proud smile.

"Now," Mike said, dropping back down on his knees. "You going to help me with this or not?"

Jack held out a leathered hand. "Yes, dear," he said, in a high falsetto. "You were saying that I hung the moon...?"

Carrie walked into her office and dropped some files on her secretary's desk. "Mary?" Carrie said, looking down at the trim young woman. "Didn't expect to find you here on a Sunday."

Mary pushed her gold wire-rim glasses up a bit higher on the bridge of her nose. "Yes, ma'am. Well, it seems that we've fallen a bit...uh, behind this week."

Carrie flushed, knowing that was because of her series of unexcused absences.

"Just here catching up."

"Great," Carrie smiled. "Me too." Since she and Mike had slept in, they'd completely missed the opportunity for the Ashton Academy reunion picnic. Yet somehow that thought hadn't mattered to either of them.

Carrie walked back to her desk, dismayed to find the pink message notes practically spilling off it. She really had been gone awhile. And now, she thought, looking down at her watch, since it was Sunday there wasn't much she could do about the phone calls. Well, there was computer work to do. And, she could check up on the stock reports, compose some letters.

Carrie plopped down in her chair, the brilliance of an idea hitting her. He hadn't mentioned it in days. But then again, in spite of her deepest desires, Carrie hadn't exactly been spouting picket fences either. Mike was just the sort of man to give up his dream for the woman he loved. But what he still didn't know was that in love, all things were possible.

"Mary," she said, calling out to her secretary. "Do we still have that old file on the Caymans?"

"Acquisition proposal?" Mary called back.

"That's the one." The thick one that contained all that research Mary'd done on property availability and Mom-and-Pop investment opportunities.

"Yes, ma'am. Got it around here somewhere. Though some of that information is bound to be dated."

"How long will it take you to correct that?"

"About twenty-four hours," Mary said, carting the heavy file over to Carrie's desk with a smile.

****

Chapter Sixteen

Mike strode purposefully into his broker's office, a broad smile on his face. "Colleen," he announced. "I'm getting married."

Colleen raised her eyebrows above the listings she was perusing but didn't look up. "That's nice." She laid down the papers and pulled a pen from her desk drawer. "Mike," she said, circling a few of the real-estate offerings detailed before her. "These are the ones I want you to call on first."

Mike stepped forward and snatched the stack off her desk. "Colleen! Didn't you hear me? I said—"

Colleen cocked her head to the side and called out in a big, bellowing tone that attracted the attention of two agents working at the copier, "Call a news conference! Send out the releases! Mike Davis is getting married..."

He glared at her.

"Again," she finished more quietly.

The other agents, a man and a woman, both junior colleagues of Mike's, went back to work with respective shrugs.

"Listen, Mike," Colleen said, clearing her throat and looking combative. Her eyes were an icy blue that matched the color of the glasses' chain around her neck. Glasses, Mike had noticed, she never seemed to wear but often seemed to look for. "Your little absences last week put us in quite a pinch here. You owe Megan and Kurt over there, and owe them big-time for picking up your slack."

Mike sank down in the chair opposite her desk, figuring now might not be the best time to ask for a raise.

"You don't watch yourself, young man, you're going to be out of a job."

Oh no. That would be even worse than failing to secure a promotion. Mike gave a pleading smile and strove to look humble. "I'm so sorry, Colleen. Really, I am. But the thing that came up last week was—unavoidable."

"Unavoidable for five days running?"

"No, I came in on Friday."

Colleen squinted.

"For half a day," Mike said, hanging his head.

She sat there waiting like a Mother Confessor.

"Listen, Colleen. Haven't you ever been in love? I mean, really in love?"

"Yes," she answered flatly. "But apparently not as many times as you have."

Mike leaned forward and accepted the real-estate listings she was extending in his direction.

"The top ones first," she said. "They need screening for an out-of-town client. And since not all of them came with pictures—"

"No problem," Mike said, standing. "I'll get on it right away."

Carrie had tossed and turned all night, excited at the prospect of her new project. But was she really doing the right thing? What if Mike hated the idea or resented her getting involved in his professional life? Unasked, no less.

Carrie looked in the mirror and tugged at her cheeks, dismayed to see the puffy bags under her eyes didn't dissipate. Maybe she should just ask him. Flat out.

But no. That would completely ruin the surprise. Carrie had seen the way his eyes had sparkled at the mention of moving to the Caymans. Once, she was certain, that had been his goal. But now, with her in the picture, could it be he was planning to put it aside? He hadn't even mentioned it since that early conversation back at the inn. Maybe he thought the idea wouldn't appeal to her.

Carrie considered how awful it would be to have something, or even somebody, unwittingly discourage your dream. Since the time she'd entered college and worked her way through, Carrie had pursued everything that was important to her. Nobody had ever told her that she couldn't. And her Grandma Russell, bless her, had always said that all she had to do was try.

Having been employed by a large New York investment firm right out of grad school, Carrie had been lucky in business. It wasn't long before she was making good money, and, because she honestly didn't have a lot of places to spend it, the money had amassed quickly. Before long, people were coming to her for favors, or opportunities for helping people just seemed to land at her feet. There was her favorite hot-dog vendor with his dream of opening up his own deli, her coworker whose aunt's independent bookstore was on the brink of foreclosure and badly needed refinancing, her apartment manager who was quite sure, if he had the funds, he could turn his dilapidated building into some of the finest condominiums on New York's Upper East side.

All of those dreams had become realities thanks to Carrie's personal investment in each of these ventures. The results had given her more than satisfaction; they had given her purpose. Within a year, she'd become incorporated and established her own independent investment firm. Two years later, she made the cover of *Forbes*. But in spite of the increasingly lucrative opportunities that poured her way, Carrie stayed true to her initial calling of helping the small businessman. Though she'd never been precisely poor, her background had been modest. And she'd seen from her own experience that a "rags to riches" existence was possible. All so many people needed was just a chance to get them started. And if the man she loved needed that same kind of chance, she would move heaven and earth to make it happen.

Carrie scooped the morning paper off her front porch and sat down to browse the financial section over coffee. She had figured Mike for some sort of real-estate venture. High-end sales, perhaps combined with property management of some of Grand Cayman's larger estates.

Carrie laid down her paper, a surprising thought taking hold. What if Mike hadn't planned to work in real estate at all in the Caymans?

But what else was there? Certainly not early retirement for a man as clever and energetic as Mike. He still seemed way too ambitious, not to mention physically...

Physical! But of course, Carrie thought with a grin. Her "swim god" wanted to go to the Caymans to capitalize on his native expertise. And Carrie wasn't talking about lovemaking... Though she was certainly hoping there'd be plenty of that.

The moment Mike stepped from the car, it hit him with a one-two punch. This was it, he thought, looking around. This was home.

The white Cape Cod was nestled in a quiet grove just west of the city. It was zoned for the best school system, one of his client's priorities, and had enough bedrooms— four—to accommodate a houseful of children.

Mike stood on the front circular drive looking up at the dormer windows protruding from the second story. Those would give plenty of light, and most likely have window seats, to the children's rooms.

When Mike stepped inside and walked through the foyer and directly to the back of the house, he was not disappointed. The high stone hearth made the open family room connecting to the kitchen look cozy. Mike's trained eye swept over the kitchen appliances, which all looked to be less than five years old. A good sign for a house that had been built in the 1940s. It was an indication the owners had routinely kept it up and not just bandaged things at the last minute for the sale.

At the back of the kitchen area sat a large bay window looking out onto immaculately tended gardens. One hosting several rows of summer vegetables, another sporting colorful flowers surrounding a sparkling pond.

Mike's heartbeat picked up a notch as he circled back through the formal living area and dining rooms, both of which needed painting but boasted gorgeous ceiling and chair-rail moldings.

Though it was his job, Mike felt surprisingly like Goldilocks as he took the stairs two at a time and hurried upstairs into the bedrooms. He went to the front of the house first, where he found, as he'd suspected, a couple of cheerfully decorated children's rooms complete with sun-dappled dormer windows.

The master bedroom was good-sized but not so large a couple could get lost in it. And the fourth bedroom, which was currently used as an office, and two upstairs baths were inviting and well maintained.

Mike felt he was bursting at the seams as he took it all in. He'd always heard buying real estate was an emotional experience. Had witnessed that enamored expression on the faces of many of his clients. But never in a million years did he dream that besotted feeling would happen to him.

Carrie would love it. He just knew it. Though her current place was charming, it was nowhere near big enough to accommodate a large family. And this house here, situated at the crest of a sleepy knoll, was not only roomy enough for plenty of children, all the rug rats Mike secretly hoped he and Carrie would make—it also afforded the same stunning view of the mountains.

Mike went downstairs and walked out onto the back patio, eyeing the one accoutrement that had cinched the deal from the moment he'd hit the property line. Fanning the border of the house's perimeter was a neat arrangement of flowers and shrubs. And behind those—gleaming in the sunlight—stood a freshly painted white picket fence.

****

Chapter Seventeen

Carrie picked up her office phone and dialed. Though she quite obviously sometimes gambled with her heart, when it came to business dealings, Carrie was exceedingly cautious. Before she went and did anything involving money, she needed to make certain her hunch was accurate.

"Hello?" Jack Davis answered.

"Jack, good morning. This is Carrie, Carrie St. John."

"Why, Carrie!" he said, sounding genuinely pleased to hear her voice. "How are you? That son of mine behaving himself? 'Cause if he's not, I'm still available, you know."

Carrie chuckled. "Oh Jack, you are bad."

"Thank you, my dear. So, what can I do for you this morning? Time to start practicing our wedding march already?"

Carrie blanched before remembering she'd impetuously invited Jack to walk her down the aisle. An act she still wasn't sorry for. Mike's dad was adorable. "Oh no, not that. But I'll certainly let you know.

"Actually, I was calling with a question—about Mike."

"Mike?" Jack exclaimed. "Well, I can't completely promise you I've figured that boy out. But go ahead and shoot, if you'd like. I'll do the best that I can."

Carrie hoped she wouldn't disillusion her prospective father-in-law by seeming too forward. But, in for a penny, in for a pound, she told herself. "It's about the British West Indies. The Cayman Islands, specifically."

Jack seemed to be waiting on the other end of the line. Not commenting, just waiting for Carrie to finish. She wasn't sure if this was good but decided to press on ahead.

"Anyhow, I realize Mike has an interest in the Caymans—"

"That so?" Jack butted in. "Didn't know he'd discussed it with you."

Ah, Carrie thought, then there was something to discuss, and something to her gut feeling after all. "Well, he mentioned it somewhat. Some time ago, actually. But I could tell, even at the time, how very important it was to him."

"I think Mike's just recently found what's most important to him."

Carrie colored at the compliment, despite the fact Jack couldn't see her. "I appreciate that, really I do. And Mike is very special to me. Extra special. I hope to marry him."

Jack was quiet for a moment before speaking. "That's wonderful! He's asked you, then?"

"Well, uh…not exactly. But let's just say I see it coming."

"Then I say, your vision's twenty-twenty, my girl."

That extra bit of reassurance warmed Carrie through and through. "But because I love him, Jack, I'd hate to think of Mike giving up any long-term dreams on my account."

"Oh, now, fluff," Jack said, huffing into the phone. "Don't you go worrying your pretty little head over that. I never really believed the boy was going to open that dive shop anyway."

Carrie hung up the phone after thanking him and promising Jack she'd let him know just as soon as they'd scheduled the wedding rehearsal. Wedding rehearsal? They still hadn't invited half the guests. The ones who would fill in the slots Wilson's missing family would have occupied.

Oh well, Carrie decided, she could think of that tomorrow. Today, she had some phone-calling to do.

"Mary," she called into the next room. "Do you have a moment to come in and make some notes?"

"Yes, ma'am," Mary said, appearing at the threshold.

"Great," Carrie said, her grin as wide as the big outdoors, "because we're slightly revising our project. Ready to dive in?"

"You sure about this?" Colleen said, staring up at Mike in disbelief. "A four-bedroom house is a big investment for a bachelor."

Mike patiently shook his head. This afternoon, not even Colleen was going to sour his mood. "Already told you, Colleen, not going to be a bachelor that much longer."

Colleen dropped into her chair in shock. "You're dead serious about this, aren't you?" For the first time for as long as he could remember, Colleen lifted the dangling bifocals from her neck and shoved them up on her nose. "Shut the door, Mike."

Mike walked to the back of Colleen's office and closed the door, giving the two of them privacy.

"Have a seat," she instructed when he returned.

"Now," Colleen said once he was seated. "Tell me honestly, what kind of trouble are you in?"

"Trouble?"

"Is the girl pregnant? Because, if she is—"

"Pregnant? Holy cow! Pregnant, Colleen?"

Colleen motioned downward with her outstretched palms. "Just calm down there, Mike. You won't be the first one on my staff who's gotten himself into a bit of a, uh...personal pickle."

"Colleen, I'm not asking you for money! I have enough for the down payment in my account. I've been saving it up for a while now for…for… Well, never mind. It's not important anymore. What is important is that I'm not asking you for any special favors here. Only the standard cut on the price based on reduced commission since someone in this office is buying it. I don't see the big deal. It's accepted protocol. I've seen you authorize such sales at least a dozen times."

"So she's not pregnant?" Colleen asked, as if she hadn't heard a word.

"Give us a couple of months," Mike said, settling back in his chair.

"How much is the house?" Colleen asked, sighing and eyeing him quizzically.

"Two-forty."

Colleen raised her eyebrows. "Joint mortgage?"

"Absolutely not," Mike told her. "This one has to be all mine." His to own and his to give away—with a full heart, Mike thought with a deep inner peace that spread from his heart to his belly.

Carrie couldn't believe her luck. There was a small store for sale just at the edge of trendy Seven Mile Beach. With all the major resort hotels nearby, the location couldn't have been more perfect. The shop, just outside of George Town, was even guaranteed docking privileges. It couldn't have been more perfect. Of course, as the store had formerly served as a knickknack-and-jewelry shop, they'd have some remodeling to do. Probably plenty of remodeling to do, given the bargain-basement price of the property, Carrie decided.

Still, if the appraiser she'd contacted at the Grand Cayman bank came back with the report Carrie expected, the place was a steal. An investment waiting to happen.

Carrie's palms moistened at the possibilities. She couldn't wait to see the look on Mike's face.

And yet, she'd have to proceed cautiously. Make certain he didn't mistake this for some kind of handout and become offended. But Carrie had never planned to give him the money, only loan it—on a long-term repayment, low-interest basis like she had for each of her other clients. It could give him the chance he needed, if he wasn't too darn proud to accept it.

Carrie paused at that last thought, considering. What if he became furious at her intrusion? What if he accused her of trying to run his life? What if he truly couldn't see that this was no sort of manipulation; it was a gift from the heart?

Carrie slouched back against her high-backed leather chair and spun to face the window. She supposed it all depended on timing. First, they had to get beyond that proposal part, so Mike wouldn't think she was trying to buy his affections. But when, oh when, was that proposal part ever going to waltz along?

Mike had said to trust him. But for how long?

She wondered if he'd even considered the wedding angle, or if he'd find using her premade arrangements tacky. To Carrie, it just seemed a terrible waste to let all that planning and expense go, just to reinvent the wheel.

Well, they would sort all of that out soon enough. First things first. She'd found the ideal property for Mike's dive shop, and if she didn't move on it quickly, somebody else would, she knew. The location was just too hot.

And, if after all her trouble, Mike hated the idea? Had completely changed his mind, and no longer wanted to move to the Caymans? Well, then, she'd just have to cross that bridge when she came to it. The shop would be a surprise, a wedding gift. And if he didn't care for it, Carrie would just have to find someone else, another entrepreneur, to take advantage of the opportunity. But that wouldn't happen. She was sure of it. Once Mike was advised of all the particulars, he was going to be over the moon.

Mike sat at his desk mooning over a picture of the house he was about to purchase and wondering how soon it would be available for occupancy. Colleen had already phoned the owners with his offer and would be letting him know that detail along with their counteroffer, when it came.

Now, if he could preoccupy—and be in within a month—that would be even better. He'd asked Colleen to inquire about the possibility. Mike couldn't wait to get started on a life with Carrie. Real stroke of luck she already had the wedding arranged. Though they hadn't talked it over officially, he guessed since he hadn't proposed "officially," Mike assumed that was what they would do. Go ahead and use the facilities and services Carrie had already arranged. She'd never canceled them, as she'd threatened to do earlier. Grandma Russell had told him so. It made his heart spring-dive just to think she'd forgone canceling those arrangements because she'd held out hope for a future with him. With him! And, holy cow, it was happening.

The house he'd found was perfect, so perfect that…

Mike stopped congratulating himself as his blood ran cold. Oh my goodness. What if he'd done the wrong thing? What if Carrie became incensed at him making such a major decision for the two of them? Without even consulting her first?

What if she didn't even want to live in Virginia but had someplace else in mind entirely? They hadn't even had a chance to discuss those kinds of future plans. Mike had just seen the house, the white picket fence and—whammy! He'd gone and done something huge, something impetuous, something nearly irrevocable. Holy cow. Mike blew a hard breath and sat back against his chair as fear settled into his belly.

Surely, Carrie wouldn't fault him for a wedding gift? Yes, that was what he'd call it. And, if she didn't like it…? Well, though they couldn't exactly return it, they could surely work something out. Find renters, resell after a while. But Mike didn't want to resell. He absolutely loved the place. And Carrie would too. He just knew it.

****

Chapter Eighteen

Carrie nervously bit into her bottom lip, smearing her lipstick against her teeth. Darn it! She'd have to start all over again. Ever since Mike had called this afternoon, she'd suspected something was up. There was an urgent expectation to his voice. No, it couldn't be tomorrow; it had to be tonight. Even though Carrie had loads to do at the office and was expected to work late, she'd come home early, showered, and put on a fresh sundress. And he wasn't even expected until seven thirty! Seven thirty. What was Carrie going to do with herself for the next forty-five minutes while waiting for him to come?

Her stomach rumbled, reminding her she should probably eat something. No, she was going to throw up. Carrie raced to the toilet, thinking she was going to lose her lunch. But after a few moments of staying still, the clench in her belly eased.

Criminy! She was a wreck. Didn't even know for certain tonight was the tonight.

Like hell she didn't, Carrie thought, racing back to the bathroom.

The telephone rang, and she limped into the bedroom to pick it up, all the while clutching her midsection.

"Darling?"

"Oh, Grandma Russell, thank goodness! I am such a wreck. Such a *wreck*. Mike called and said—"

"Hold on there, child. Slow down. Can't make out a word you're saying."

"I'm, um…" Carrie sat down on the bed and started to cry. "Oh Grandma, I've never wanted anything more in my life."

"Calm down. Just take a deep, deep breath."

Carrie inhaled.

"Now let it out."

She did.

"Go on, a few more times. In and out. I'm not going anywhere; I can wait."

Carrie wiped the moisture from her cheeks and sat up a little straighter.

"Now, you still with me?" her grandmother asked. "Or should I call the rescue squad?"

Carrie let out a laugh that released more tears. But this time, she felt more in control. "Thanks, Grandma," she said, taking another deep breath. "You're the best."

"What's all this about wanting? You mean the dang hunk hasn't proposed by now?"

"Not yet, but it's coming," Carrie said, holding out her trembling left hand and examining the bare ring finger. "I can feel it. Just like that musky heat right before a rain."

"Well," Grandma Russell said, "he's been waiting for a reason. So don't you go jumping all over him with kisses and I-do's before he can get two words out. First, give the rascal a chance to say his piece."

"Jumping…? Why, Grandma Russell, what do you take me for, an impatient woman?"

Her grandma chuckled. "Just a woman who knows what she wants. And I can't say I blame you. He is a dish, that Mike Davis, he is."

"Grandmother! It's not all about the way he looks, and you know it!"

"Yes, I know. But I also know enough to know looks don't hurt. Especially when the man in question looks just like a young Robert—"

"There you go with that movie-star thing again. I swear, that's not helping."

Grandma Russell hooted. "I can't wait for the big day. It will be so nice feeling like you are finally anchored in Virginia, Carrie love. I just know with that man of yours at home, those week-long trips to New York won't seem nearly as enticing."

Carrie thought about telling her but decided against it. Why spoil her grandmother's jovial mood? Besides, Carrie was finally feeling better herself. Perhaps if she had some yogurt and a bit of soda. She definitely needed something in her stomach, and the soda would help her queasies.

"I think I'd better go and grab something to eat before he gets here," Carrie said, standing and walking to the kitchen. "Keep those fingers crossed for me."

"Absolutely," Grandma Russell reported, "and all my lavender-painted toes."

Carrie hung up the phone, wondering if her grandmother had really painted her toenails purple or was just being funny. With Grandma Russell, one never really knew. Perhaps expressly why Grandpa Russell married her in the first place.

Okay, Mike told himself, scooping the brand-new engagement ring off his carpet for the third time. This wasn't good. Not good at all. He was all thumbs tonight. What a wonderful night to propose. Plus, it was predicted to rain. How romantic. He had planned to take Carrie to his special spot, right there in Norton Vineyards. He'd even bought a Norton Sweet Virginia Red and a whole box of mint chocolate chip ice cream sandwiches to complement the evening.

Before, when he'd acted rashly and proposed to the wrong women, he'd charted a course for disaster. Not this time. Not this time, indeed. Tonight was special. Carrie was special. And the dag-blasted ring he'd traded for Alexia's had cost only a few hundred more. A few hundred, but worth every dime.

Yet the custom setting Mike had arranged had taken time. An unsettling amount of time. On a couple of occasions, in fact, Mike had actually feared Carrie was going to propose to him instead, if he didn't hurry it up.

Well, now all that was neither here nor there because he had the ring, he thought, wedging it back in its box and shoving it down in his pocket. He walked to the kitchen counter, completing his mental checklist. He had the wine. Check. He felt his other pocket for the Swiss Army knife with the corkscrew. Check. And the ice cream… He opened the freezer to find it bare.

Mike whirled on his heels toward the center of the kitchen where a soggy brown-paper bag wilted against the table. Holy cow! Not again. But it was, in fact. Even worse than the first time.

Carrie fiddled with her watch and paced the living room. She picked up the remote and switched on the television. News and game shows. She switched it off again.

She checked the mantel clock. Seven forty-five. All right, Carrie, she told herself, fifteen minutes late does not a disaster make. He could be running a bit behind, could have stopped for gas.

Carrie felt like she was getting a sick headache. No, not tonight, she prayed. Not tonight of all nights. She went to the kitchen and poured some water from the tap, preparing to take two aspirin, when a firm knock sounded at the front door.

Carrie's stomach revolted.

She raced to the door and tugged it open, just before making a beeline for the bathroom. Carrie slammed the door at her back and fell to her knees.

Mike trailed Carrie to the bathroom, only to have the door slammed in his face. Poor thing, she looked positively awful. White as a sheet. Holy cow. What was happening here?

Mike tapped lightly at the door. "Carrie? Honey, you all right?"

"Fine, fine," she muttered through running water. But she sounded less than perfect.

Mike looked down at the two bags clutched in his hands, thinking that neither the new ice cream he'd just picked up nor the wine would look too appealing to Carrie at the moment.

After a few minutes of silence, he tried knocking again. "Carrie?"

Finally, she pulled back the door, looking ghostly.

"Oh sweetie," Mike said, "come over here and sit down. You don't look so hot."

She gave him a twisted smile, remembering the first time he'd said that. "Bet you say that to all the girls."

"No," he said, depositing his bags on the coffee table and sitting beside her on the sofa. "Actually, it's just the opposite…" He reached out and took her hands in his. "Is it the flu? Did it hit suddenly?"

"You could say that," she answered, smiling past her queasiness.

"Stay put," he said, releasing her hands and giving her knee a light pat. "I'll go and get you some ginger ale."

"What did you bring me?" she asked when he returned from the kitchen and handed her the glass.

Mike followed her gaze to the two paper grocery bags on the table. "Probably nothing you'd feel much like having now. How about I tuck them in the fridge?"

Carrie nodded and took a very slow, small sip from her glass.

Mike shook his head as he stored the wine and ice cream in the refrigerator. Sick? She was sick? After everything he had planned—rehearsed—to make this night perfect? Holy cow.

Just when he thought things couldn't possibly get any worse, Mike heard the hard rhythm of rain beating against the kitchen window.

Carrie wanted to curl up into a ball and die. Whatever he'd planned... All the trouble he'd gone to, and now she couldn't even lift herself off the sofa. This was not the way she'd envisioned things at all. Maybe she was jinxed, or perhaps she'd already gotten her fair share of uneventful proposals. Whatever the reason, she was damned upset it was happening to her now.

Carrie glanced up toward the ceiling, hearing a sound smacking the red-slate roof. Perfect, it was raining.

"Penny for your thoughts?" Mike said, coming back over to the sofa and sitting beside her.

"Oh Mike," she said, her voice breaking up, "I'm so sorry..."

"Hush," he said, bringing a hand to her lips and gently stroking her chin. "You can't help any more that you're sick than I can the color of my eyes."

Oh, she wished she could believe it. But no, she felt responsible. As if the whole disastrous evening, one that could have been the most memorable ever for the two of them, was all her fault. If only she hadn't worked herself into such a tizzy. If only she'd had a regular dinner. If only...

"Carrie," Mike said, laying a hand on her forearm. "How do you think the air would do you?"

"Air?" she asked, not understanding.

"I was thinking of the porch swing."

Carrie agreed that it was a fine idea and that being outdoors might actually help her. So she accepted Mike's assistance and leaned on him heavily as he helped her outside and onto the porch swing, all the while thinking that this was how life would be. The two of them leaning on each other, growing old together. Each one forever supporting the other.

Carrie felt the moisture on her cheek and raised a casual hand to her eye, hoping Mike hadn't seen. He already thought she was falling apart. Why give him further proof?

"Need a blanket?" he asked as a heavy gust of wind dusted a spray of rain in their direction.

"Just your arm," she said, smiling up at him.

Mike sat and wrapped his arm around her, scooting in close. Carefully, slowly, when he felt her capable of tolerating the motion, Mike sent the swing into a gentle rock.

Far away, the mountains dripped and bled color in the evening rain. And, closer at hand, an occasional whistling wind across fresh flowers sent lazy summer fragrances wafting onto the porch. Mike held her and stroked her shivering arm until it steadied in his warmth.

Brushstrokes of light streaked into blackness in the darkening sky as her head dropped against his shoulder in easy comfort and they continued to rock. And when she grew heavy and still, Mike knew that she'd fallen asleep.

It was just like the dancing. And he wanted it to go on and on and on… Yes, he was sorry about the evening and his lost opportunity for fulfilling plans. But he was doubly grateful for the chance just to hold her now, with nothing but the scent of the rain between them. If this snapshot was an indication of the next sixty years, Mike was awfully glad he'd seen the big picture early.

Carrie awoke with a start to see the sun peering over the purple mountains. It was only when she heard the low rumble that she realized Mike was sitting and snoring beside her.

"Mike?" she said, raising a hand to his face. "Mike?"

"I'd like to counter that offer," he said, snapping to attention.

"What offer?" she asked, laughing in surprise. "Were you dreaming about real estate?"

Mike opened his eyes wide, then blinked at his surroundings. "Yeah, I guess that I was," he said, rubbing the sore back of his neck. "Did we sleep here all night?"

"Unless little trolls carried us to my bed, then replaced us on the swing before sunup."

Mike pulled her into his arms and nuzzled her neck. "You know," he said, "that's the first time I've ever done that. Pulled an all-nighter with a woman on a swing."

Carrie smiled, enjoying his warmth, enjoying the new day. Savoring the implausibility of the moment. And thinking that she'd happily wake up with Mike Davis anywhere.

"You stick with me, and you'll get lots more opportunities for firsts," she said, feeling playful. And, thank goodness, so much better.

"You're looking brighter this morning," he said, stroking her cheek. "I was so sorry to see you so ill."

"Thanks for staying with me. Being with you really helped."

Mike turned to the woman beside him. All night on the porch after an evening of illness, and Carrie St. John was without a doubt the most beautiful women he'd ever seen. The only woman with whom he could envision sharing a lifetime.

"Think you could get used to it?" Mike asked, moving his hands to her shoulders and looking deep in her eyes.

Carrie nodded but didn't say a word. Because her heart was on fire. She knew, unmistakably, what was coming next. But this time, Carrie wasn't anxious or afraid. Every nerve ending was ready.

Mike slipped out of the rocker and got down on one knee.

"Carrie," he said, taking her left hand in both of his. "I have something very important to ask you. And just so you know, I want to tell you I already did the proper thing and talked with your grandmother."

"Yes!" Carrie said, springing off the porch swing and into his arms as he stood in surprise to catch her. "Yes, yes, oh Mike, yes," she said between vibrant kisses that ran from his mouth to his cheek to his neck to his forehead.

"Carrie—" he said, stopping her when she was almost to his mouth again. "You didn't even let me finish asking."

"Oh," she said, consumed by a groundswell of heat. "Sorry." Carrie primly smoothed out her hair and sat back down on the swing. "Continue," she said, looking up, a million constellations in her eyes.

Mike smiled to beat all get-out and pulled a ring box from his pocket. "Before I say what I have to say," he told her while her heart beat fiercely with anticipation, "I want you to promise me you'll keep that level of enthusiasm for the next say, oh…fifty to sixty years."

"It's a deal," she said with a sexy grin that almost made him drop the box and cart her straight inside.

"Carrie St. John," Mike said, dropping back down on one knee, half wondering if he might get tackled. He pulled back the velvet lid, revealing a beautiful blue diamond surrounded by six perfect rubies.

"Oh Mike…"

"I'm sorry it took a while, but this ring was sort of a symbolic gift. I wanted to get it just right."

Carrie wrinkled her brow as Mike plucked the ring from its box.

"The diamond… Well, of course, you know what the diamond means, love everlasting and all that." He grinned, and she shot him a look with her eyes that dazzled.

"And the rubies?" Carrie asked. She counted. "Six of them?"

"Well, these first two," Mike said, pointing to the stones set at the top. "These are you and me."

Carrie's eyes watered.

"Because, well…" He looked at her and smiled. "I figured out some time ago that you and I are—two of a kind. Destined for each other. Meant to be."

Carrie swallowed hard past the lump in her throat. "And the others?"

He gave her a hopeful smile, green eyes glistening. "Jack, Amanda, little Carrie, and Mike Junior," he said, touching the stones one by one with his right index finger.

Salty tears streamed from Carrie's eyes. Amanda was her Grandma Russell's name, though how Mike had known, she couldn't fathom.

"Of course, if you don't like those names, we could choose others," he said, reaching up and wiping her cheeks.

"I love those names. But…four?" she said, her voice warbling.

"For starters, anyway," Mike said with a Cheshire-cat grin as he slipped the ring on her finger. "Carrie St. John," he said, looking into her deep-brown eyes, "will you be mine, to have, to hold, and to cherish from this day forward...?"

Carrie nodded and kissed his hands still holding her own. "Oh, I will. I will, I will, I will!" She smiled, giving the morning sun a run for its money. "But...Mike, I kind of think you're supposed to save those words for the wedding."

"The wedding?" Mike asked, pulling her up and into his arms. Right where she belonged. Torso to torso, heart to thundering heart.

"But that's only six days away," he said, closing in for a kiss. "Shouldn't we start practicing up?"

What, oh what, was she going to do with this man?

Keep him, she supposed.

"Absolutely," Carrie said as she kissed him back, and he swept her away.

****

Epilogue

After a private ceremony and small family reception, featuring mint-chocolate wedding cake, Mike took Carrie on a long country drive, after which he surprised her by carting her over the threshold of a darling Cape Cod with a white picket fence. After crying several million tears and drinking the sweet Virginia wine Mike had stocked in the fridge, Carrie told him about his new investment opportunity in the Caymans.

Once they'd gotten over the initial shock of just how alike they truly were, the delighted couple arrived at a happy compromise. They would rent out the new house for a year while they lived on Grand Cayman and got Mike's dive-shop business off the ground. Afterward, they would settle back in Virginia and begin fulfilling Carrie's engagement-ring promise of creating four beautiful children.

So they could keep an eye on him, Mike's father, Jack, would be invited to join them in the islands for that first year. They would rent him someplace scenic, not too far from their own home, where he could watch the saucy Caribbean sun stretching its long fingers over the morning waters—and enjoy the personal attentions of his own private nurse.

Once back in Virginia, they'd continue to vacation on Grand Cayman, and Mike would make occasional business trips, as needed, to check up on his shop. Then eventually, once Mike found the perfect piece of real estate, they'd build a breezy getaway on the island's east end and summer there on a regular basis.

And while they plotted, planned, and worked out all these intimate details, the newlyweds, Mr. and Mrs. Michael John Davis, sat on the front steps of their perfect new home and ate a whole box of ice cream sandwiches—before they melted.

The End

A Note from the Author

Thanks for reading *The Sometime Bride*. I hope you enjoyed it. If you did, please help other people find this book.

1. This book is lendable, so loan it to a friend who you think might like it so that she (or he) can discover me, too.

2. Help other people find this book: write a review.

3. Sign up for my newsletter so that that you can learn about the next book as soon as it's available. Write to GinnyBairdRomance@gmail.com with "newsletter" in the subject heading.

4. Come like my Facebook page: http://www.facebook.com/GinnyBairdRomance.

Look for the first two books in my "Girls on the Go" series, *Santa Fe Fortune* and *How to Marry a Matador*. Available in print and online now.

Interested in seeing an extended excerpt from *Santa Fe Fortune?* Please keep reading for more.

****

Dear Readers,

It is with pleasure and passion that I introduce my "Girls on the Go" series with this launch book, *Santa Fe Fortune.* When I was a young college woman, I studied abroad in beautiful Seville, Spain. I was at an impressionable age to experience new things, including my first deeply felt love. And, while I developed a significant and memorable romance, the most profound discovery I made that year was the unveiling of myself. For it is often in distancing ourselves from what is most familiar that we truly come to understand ourselves.

With these thoughts in mind, I conceived this new book series, designed to showcase powerful yet evolving heroines enduring journeys of the heart while traveling far from home. So please, pack up your suitcase and join us for the adventure. I discovered Santa Fe, New Mexico last summer, and promptly fell in love. Both with the charming city, and—once again—with my wonderful husband John. *Such a lovely spot for romance,* I found myself thinking. And then, being a writer… Well, the ideas for this story started flowing.

I like Gwen a lot. She's a genuine gal, who's been through rough times and deserves real happiness. She might not be perfect, but she just might be perfect for precisely the right man. In any case, Gwen's sure to appreciate what the future heroines in this series will also learn: it's who you are on the inside that matters. Once you believe in your strengths, others will see them too.

With best wishes for happy endings,

Ginny Baird, author of "Girls on the Go"

Sometimes you have to get away to find yourself!

SANTA FE FORTUNE

"I had a really great time tonight," she said, beaming up at him and feeling very much as if it had been a date.

"Me too," he said, stepping a fraction of an inch closer. Sea-blue eyes washed over her, threatening to pull her under. And boy, did she want to get swept away. *"I'm glad you agreed to see me tomorrow, even if it's just an arrangement."*

Gwen sensed Dan could rearrange her heart every which way, if she wasn't careful. *"I'm glad I'm seeing you too,"* she said, feeling the warmth in her cheeks.

"Ten o'clock work for you?" he asked, his tone growing gravelly.

"Uh-huh," she uttered, mesmerized by his gaze.

He moved nearer now, his mouth just inches away. *"I'll be damned if I don't want to kiss you,"* he said, his voice a husky rasp.

And she'd be damned if she didn't want him to. *"Dan..."* she said, tilting up her chin and closing her eyes.

"But I won't," he said, snapping her back to attention, eyes open. *"Not now. Not here. Not like this..."*

She started to speak as he brought his fingers to her lips. *"If ever I've seen a woman who deserves to be kissed well, it's you. But the timing has got to be right. You have to be sure."* He cast a cursory glance at her wedding band and backed away. *"I need to be sure. Something tells me we've both gone down a path neither of us wants to travel again..."*

****

Chapter One

Gwendolyn Marsh leaned across the large oak table that served as a desk. "I'm going to be honest with you, Mr. Holbrook. I didn't fly all the way out here to get swindled."

Dan stared in disbelief at the incredibly contentious woman. *Swindled* was an awfully big accusation coming from such a small frame. She couldn't stand more than five foot five in heels, and she'd nearly tumbled off them striding into the place.

"Like I told you, Mrs. Marsh, I'm not in the position to make that decision. If two thousand a canvas is what Ms. Holstein quoted you in the email, then I'm afraid I'll need to stick by that."

Soft gold curls fell at uneven angles, framing a lovely face as deep brown eyes homed in on him. If she weren't so hard-edged, he might consider her beautiful. Dan stopped himself, realizing appraisals of the clientele weren't in his job description.

"It's *Ms.,* if you must know."

Some lucky fellow was off the hook.

"My apologies. I saw the wedding band and…"

"It's a relic, okay? I haven't gotten used to going without it."

"I'm sorry, I had no idea. I understand it takes a while."

She leveled him a look, as if he were the culprit. Hey, maybe in her eyes, all men were. Dan had met the type before and could easily read the signs: *steer clear, not for you buddy, a sexy woman's not everything…* Sexy? Did he just think *sexy?* Gwendolyn Marsh wasn't movie-star thin like most females here. Her formfitting sundress hugged every curve in just the right way. Wrong way, as far as he was concerned. This was just another sign he'd been alone too long. It wasn't like Dan didn't have his reasons. In fact, when he was being honest, Dan realized he was likely worse news for her than she was for him. All women after a while had hopes, dreams…and Dan Holbrook was just the man to dash them.

Dark eyes sparked with fierce determination. "I think I'd like to speak to Ms. Holstein myself."

"I'm afraid that won't be possible."

She arched one perfectly manicured eyebrow. "Why not?"

This was just what Dan needed, a hot-tempered, hot-bodied woman waltzing into his Santa Fe gallery on a hot July afternoon. Okay, it wasn't technically his gallery…

Dan cursed himself for his soft spot in agreeing to run the place while Nancy was away. He didn't even like being indoors.

"Ms. Holstein is in the south of France, will be until next month."

She pulled her naturally plump lips into a thin pink line. "I see." She faltered slightly, nearly losing her composure. There was sheen to her eyes that made them look moist. Dan hoped she wasn't about to break down crying. Nancy had assured him this would be easy, just a few clients flying in from out of state. Surprise negotiations and weepy women weren't in the mix. Negotiations Dan could handle. Weepy women were another story.

A bell tinkled above the door, and a couple of well-dressed patrons entered, a man in an expensive suit and a woman wearing a tailored dress and high-end cowgirl boots.

"Be right with you folks," Dan told them, surmising these were the buyers from Los Angeles.

Gwen stood, apparently taking this as a dismissal. "Well, I guess that's it, then." She tucked her clutch under one arm and thrust forward the opposite hand. "Thanks for your time."

Dan sent a furtive glance at the Californians perusing shelves of New Mexican pottery and pretending not to listen. "Ms. Marsh, I'm afraid we got off on the wrong…" She tapped a strappy sandal, sporting bright painted nails and multiple toe rings. Heat rose at Dan's nape as his gaze eased up shapely legs. "…foot."

She withdrew her hand and cocked her head sideways, waiting.

"What I mean is, please sit back down, and let's discuss this like reasonable people. I'm sure we can work something out." Dan cringed at the sound of his own voice. Groveling? Here was a word not even in his vocabulary, yet he was being just about as placating as humanly possible. Dan wasn't doing it for himself, he remembered. He was doing this for Nancy. Other than the day-to-day oversight of things, which really was no problem, she'd given him only two jobs to do. Surely a man as capable at cutting deals as he was wouldn't have trouble selling a few items to some Los Angeles industry execs and buying canvases from an easy-going North Carolina native. Dan had a notion Nancy had never met Gwendolyn Marsh face-to-face when she'd made the latter assessment.

The hardness lining her eyes eased just a little. "I suppose I could stay for a bit," she said, her voice taking on the lilt of the mid-Atlantic South. She took her seat, splaying the lap of her flowered sundress across tightly nestled knees.

The Californians tastefully removed themselves to the back of the gallery to study a photographic desert landscape series, and Dan sat as well. He plucked a hanky from his suit pocket and dabbed the back of his neck, thinking it had to be over a hundred degrees in here.

Something tender welled in Dan's throat, and he realized he wasn't just doing this for Nancy. For some inexplicable reason, he felt driven to be nice to Ms. Marsh for her own sake. Never mind that she'd practically bulldozed right over him crashing in here. After all, he'd dealt with worse in business before. The truth was Nancy had given him some leeway. If Marsh really pushed, Dan could go up as high as three thousand a pop, mostly because Nancy had faith in Marsh's work and thought it was good. Nancy also believed that Marsh could develop a Santa Fe following. Many of the buyers here came from the West Coast, and Marsh's oils capturing snippets of sea life would be a ready sell. Dan had seen the slides, and they were impressive. Borrowing more from impressionism than realism, Marsh had a way of zeroing in on the smallest, seemingly inconsequential detail, like an isolated seashell, and illuminating it in a special and grandiose way.

She opened her purse and withdrew a thin ledger. "If you'd let me show you my figures, I'm sure you'll understand why my prices have gone up."

Dan scanned the haphazardly arranged numbers, deciding she was no mathematician. He pointed to one clumsily assumed total. "I can understand where material costs have climbed, but how exactly is it that your hourly rate has doubled?"

"Hard times, Mr. Holbrook," she said without flinching. "Don't you read the papers?"

"*Wall Street Journal* and you?" he bantered without skipping a beat.

"Well, I…read, of course." With that, she awkwardly angled an elbow and sent her clutch crashing to the floor. "Oh no!"

A small cloud of makeup powder-puffed up from beneath them as a rolling lipstick assaulted Dan's loafer. To this day, he'd never understood the mysteries of a woman's bag.

"Here, let me," he began.

"No! I've got it!"

They bent simultaneously toward the mound of sprawled purse contents, nearly knocking heads. "I'm sorry!" he said, down on hands and knees to help her.

"My fault!"

A scent overtook him as cunning and fine as the most succulent desert flower. Dan looked up into bewitching brown eyes less than six inches away. Whatever was happening here, he had to put a halt to it. This was no sensible way for a man pushing forty to behave. He was reeling like a raving teenager. He hadn't been in a position this compromising with a woman in a while, and it showed. All sorts of crazy thoughts went racing through his head, like how it might feel to kiss her good and hard as she probably deserved.

"You guys okay over there?" a pair of cowgirl boots called from the corner.

"Thanks, we've got it!" Gwen replied, scooting back on her knees. She couldn't believe this mess! What had she gotten herself into? Here she was with this hunky beast of a man, trapped beneath a solid yet decorative desk.

He had a rugged face, tanned like he was used to working outdoors. His sandy hair held a hint of sunlight too. Toned muscles strained beneath his suit jacket as he posed on all fours, looking far more like a predator in the wild than a staid art collector. Gwen had an improbable instinct to flee but was powerless to run away. He'd been an impossible man above board, but down here in the shadows, he revealed something more. Instinct told Gwen that Holbrook was the sort of man who knew how to kiss a woman and kiss her right. She imagined getting swept into his powerful arms, his mouth moving down on hers...

"Are you all right?" His gaze dove into her as heat crept up her cheeks.

"Yes, fine. That's all, I think," she said, scooping the remainders into her clutch.

Gwen didn't know why his gorgeous stare had unnerved her so. It wasn't like she was attracted to him, for heaven's sake. If her take on Holbrook was correct, he had plenty of women falling all over him already. What would a sophisticated Western entrepreneur like him want with a Carolina girl like her anyway? Apart from a quick good time, probably not a lot, and Gwendolyn Marsh was quite done with being somebody's goodtime girl, thank you very much.

Little lines pulled at the corners of his mouth, and she realized suddenly they were still both on the floor. "If you've got all you need, don't you think we should..." He gave a thumbs-up, and she pushed back, standing awkwardly.

Holbrook brushed off his trousers, the slight tugs showing off powerfully muscled thighs. Clearly not just a gallery owner, she thought, cheeks flaming as he caught her staring.

A tense moment ensued as both appeared to forget where they were or what they were there for. As if to remind them, the California man loudly cleared his throat.

"Just finishing up," Dan told him. "Ms. Marsh," he began, addressing her.

"Gwen, please. I'd be happy if you called me Gwen." She smoothed the wrinkles from her dress and straightened the neckline.

"Gwen," he said, offering up his first true smile since she'd arrived, and boy, was it a winner. If a heartbreaker contest existed in all of the Southwest, Gwen would bet on Holbrook to take the prize. "I'm afraid I've already taken up too much of your time."

Gwen spied the California couple circling closer like sharks, apparently having grown tired of waiting, and panic set in. What a terrible two days she'd had. First, her flight to Atlanta was delayed. Then, she'd missed her Albuquerque connection, causing her to miss her originally scheduled gallery appointment. To top it off, when she finally got a replacement flight, she'd chipped a nail stuffing her bulging carry-on into the overhead compartment.

Making Santa Fe from the airport last night was easy. Finding the craftily concealed entity of Holbrook and Holstein on Canyon Road this morning proved more elusive. Even her GPS was miffed, telling her to make legal U-turns wherever possible, no matter that the prospect involved going round and round in the Vegan Market parking lot.

Now, after making a wreck of this business call, she'd be leaving here having done no business at all. Not one sale to the gallery, despite her tumultuous flight and anxiety-producing encounter with Dan Holbrook.

Gwen pulled herself up a little straighter and squared her small shoulders. She couldn't leave New Mexico without getting what she came for. Too many people depended on her, and this was the one shot she had.

"Maybe we can continue this conversation later?" she asked with a hopeful twist to her lips.

"I was just about to suggest that."

"You were?" she asked with surprise.

"Ms. Marsh…" He stopped himself. "Gwen… Do you really think Holbrook and Holstein would have had you come all this way if we didn't have a genuine interest in your work?" Crinkles formed at the corners of his blue eyes, and Gwen's heart soared.

"But I thought you said the prices quoted to me in the email were…"

"Everything in life is negotiable. Well, almost everything. Tell you what, why don't you give me a few hours to put through a phone call to France, and I'll see what I can do."

In an instant, Gwen retracted every uncharitable thought she'd had about him. When she'd first walked into the swanky, upscale warehouse and spied him double-checking the pricing on a large wall weaving, she'd imagined him incredibly stuck-up. Who wouldn't be with that six-foot build and well-proportioned frame that spoke of power and unerring self-control? She'd pegged him as the rigid sort who never took no for an answer and considered his own words the final determinant. Now that he was showing a small sliver of humanity, she realized she might have misjudged him.

"I'd love to talk again," she said, meaning it sincerely. "When's best for you?"

"How about tomorrow at lunch? Will that work?"

Ms. Holstein, his business partner, Gwen presumed, had proposed that Gwen make a little vacation out of her stay in Santa Fe while she was at it. Her sister Marian had thought it was a fine idea too. *"Go for it, Gwen! Now's your chance to finally get away!"* What Marian didn't know, and Gwen hadn't been prepared to tell her, was that Gwen's coming to Santa Fe had a whole lot to do with her.

"I'm booked at the inn for ten days," she said, smiling softly. "So, lunch tomorrow is fine."

Holbrook surprised her with a smile of his own. "Awesome." He nabbed a gallery card and quickly penned something on the back. "Let's meet here. Something tells me the conversation might flow a little better between us given a couple of avocado margaritas."

"Avocado?" she retorted, half stunned, half horrified.

Holbrook gave a genuine chuckle as she accepted his card. "Nobody's forcing the hard stuff on you. I'm sure there will be tea and soda available too."

There was a twinkle in his eye that set her tailbone tingling. Slow down there, sister, Gwen told herself. This is strictly business now. Not anywhere near a date.

"What time?" she asked primly, pinning her clutch to her side.

He studied her in an amused way. "One o'clock okay?"

"One sounds fine!" she said, scurrying toward the exit before she could do or say something absurd.

"Watch the…!"

Gwen spun toward him, noting she'd nearly upset a pretty, handblown glass vase with the edge of her bag. She grimaced, slinking out the door as the gaping Californians gawked on.

Once outside and beyond sight of the gallery's windows, Gwen snatched her bag from beneath her arm and whacked herself soundly on the forehead. Stupid, stupid, stupid. She might have blown the whole thing. And not just by breaking a priceless piece of art. The way she'd started things out had been nothing short of shameless. Crafting a confrontation with the primary gallery owner. Clearly, that could lead to nothing but butting heads.

Gwen felt a warmth surge through her, recalling their close encounter of the nearly carnal kind. There was more to Dan Holbrook than met the eye. Hadn't he just proved that with his turn of kindness at the end? But the truth of the matter was that whatever sort of man he was, or wasn't, was beside the point. Gwen had come to Santa Fe on a mission, and that mission involved dollar signs. She didn't just want the money; she needed it. Twenty thousand in cash, and she wasn't leaving New Mexico without it.

Dan finished business quickly with the couple from Los Angeles after offering sincere apologies for making them wait. They'd prearranged to purchase the desert photo series, and everything, including price negotiations, thank goodness, had been settled with Nancy in advance. It was a simple matter of the pair presenting a check and Dan providing the receipt. In the morning, he'd arrange for shipping, and Nancy's gallery assistant would be in to help with the details. That would be the simple part of Dan's day. Lunchtime could prove more problematic.

Dan chided himself for suggesting Gwen meet him at La Cantina rather than here. Outwardly, he told himself that he was being charitable. Gwen had seemed so uptight at the gallery, perhaps a more comfortable venue would be less intimidating. He'd read her résumé and understood that if she sold through Holbrook and Holstein, it would be her first real sale, her official launch in the art world. But deep in the veiled recesses of his soul, Dan suspected a slight ulterior motive. He hadn't enjoyed the company of an attractive woman in ages, and this was a safe way to do it. Lunch in the middle of the day, a straightforward business deal? What could be more innocent? Raw doubts niggled at him as he warned himself against getting in too deep. The way he'd sprung the invitation on Gwen had been completely out of character. It had been a split-second decision, an act on impulse, and Dan was anything but an impulsive man.

He would never have built his empire of custom-design homes for the moneyed set if he'd operated from a basis of anything but collected cool. In those circles, Dan was known for his keen eye and level head, as well as his effectiveness in putting together a team. From the highest-level architect to the most basic yet very skilled carpenter, every one of Holbrook Designs' workers was treated with utmost respect and handsomely paid. This was particularly appreciated in the current economic climate but had always been the operational mode for Dan. Whether times were easy or hard, Dan's business remained steady. While his homes certainly weren't cheap, they were of a consistent quality the buyer could count on. Plus, Dan was a man of his word who stood by his product. People could depend on him to deliver the best and ensure they had a comfortable and stunningly beautiful place in which to live for years to come. It was an area in which Dan felt confident, competent.

This temporary gallery-running made him feel something altogether different, and Dan didn't like it one bit. While working with the California couple had gone fine, dealing with Ms. Gwendolyn Marsh had thrown him unexpectedly off-kilter. Nancy had nowhere near prepared him for that. Just because he'd helped his big sister finance this place, that didn't mean he wanted to be involved in any intimate way. Nancy was the art history major who loved the ins and outs of acquiring art. Running a gallery in Santa Fe had always been her dream, and once Dan had found himself in a position to help with that, he'd been more than happy to foot the bill. He'd never imagined that she'd repay him by listing his name as the primary gallery owner. This perpetually led to confusion, like during his exchange with Gwen today.

No matter. He'd straighten all that out tomorrow. Surely, after a good lunch and some cordial conversation, they'd arrive at a fair compromise on price. It would be a simple matter to smooth over during coffee and dessert. Then Ms. Gwendolyn Marsh could cart her sexy little tail all the way back to North Carolina, and Dan would continue counting down the days to Nancy's return, when he would once again be free to retreat to the peaceful quiet of Paradise Ranch. Life wasn't really so complicated after all, Dan decided, thinking it through. All you needed was a plan. And Dan's plans didn't include one firecracker of a Southern belle upending his world and sending his foolish heart racing. For Dan Holbrook, days like that were done. His throat ached at the memory. He swallowed hard, trying to force it back down. Dan had stepped into the fire once and had come out barbequed. No need to start poking at coals again.

Gwen sat on the patio of her airy suite, surrounded by sweeping adobe walls, potted ferns, and cactus flowers. Despite the record-high temperatures, the lack of humidity made it pleasant enough to stay outdoors in the shade. She sipped at her host's complimentary glass of chardonnay, knowing she needed to be cautious. At seven thousand feet above sea level, one glass of wine could feel like two. The inn's cocktail hour had also offered a selection of fruits, vegetables, and cheeses, and Gwen had fixed herself a small plate as a buffering against the booze. She'd have to remain mindful of herself tomorrow at lunch, particularly in light of the proposed margaritas.

Gwen couldn't help but feel a slight tingle of hopeful anticipation. For the first time in as long as she remembered, she'd be eating out with an eligible man. She knew, of course, that it was just an art deal, and she was merely passing through town. It was nonetheless hard to deny the tiniest fluttering in her tummy that sprang to life each time she recalled being face-to-face on the floor with the undeniably handsome Holbrook. Had something authentic actually passed between them, or had Gwen been so nervous and delusional as to have imagined the whole thing?

She glanced down at the simple gold band on her left ring finger. Gwen wasn't sure if it was her marriage she couldn't forget or her failure to maintain it. *"Marshes aren't quitters!"* her mom, Elizabeth, had always said. While life may have quit on Elizabeth, she wasn't about to let her daughters give up on anything. It was a mantra burned into them, her and her sister Marian both. Gwen only wished Marian had quit having babies about three children ago. Marian was expecting her sixth, and after years of verbal and physical abuse, her alcoholic husband, Tom, had finally run out on her. Gwen had truthfully considered this a blessing, as it had been clear after the first couple of years that Marian never intended to leave Tom.

Marian worked part-time as a hospital nurse and tried to get the day shift as much as possible. When she was gone, she left her oldest, the eleven-year-old, in charge. During night shifts, her elderly neighbor, Ms. Tilly, helped out. During the academic year, Marian had daycare arranged for the twins while the others were in school. She wasn't sure how she'd manage once the new baby came along, especially under the threat of losing her home. Marian's mortgage was several months overdue, and the collectors were moving in. She hadn't told Gwen that Tom stopped sending payments, or that she was in so deep, until it was almost too late. As it was, Marian barely had funds in her meager savings account to buy a few months' worth of diapers. Her checking account was essentially empty, being worn down month after month by her family's needs, including the kids' doctors' bills.

Marian had been in tears when she'd told Gwen the truth. If she lost her house, she feared her children would be taken away from her. She had nowhere else to go. Gwen's sparse two-bedroom could scarcely hold them all, not for any length of time, at least. And their mom, having long ago been placed in the memory-care unit of a retirement home, was far from being able to help. She barely scraped by on Social Security and most days didn't recognize either of her daughters, besides.

If Marian could just hang on one more year until the twins were in school, she thought she could make it. With only the new baby to place in daycare, she'd be able to work full-time. That would give her benefits like a retirement pension and health insurance. She'd be better able to meet her kids' medical expenses as well as plan for her own future. As it stood, she had six months of back mortgage to pay and another twelve months' obligation to look forward to. She was overwhelmed and in pieces, unsure of what to do. Taking Tom to court wasn't an option. Marian didn't have the financial resources, and even if she did, it would be hard squeezing blood from a stone. Tom was on and off the bottle and in and out of work. She couldn't rely on him now any more than she had during their marriage.

It was a dire and depressing situation. Gwen had thought for weeks about what she might do to help her sister. The trouble was Gwen was in financial strife herself. Robert had been so furious at her for kicking him out, he'd run up over ten thousand dollars in credit-card debt on purpose. The pro bono women's shelter attorney Gwen consulted said there was nothing Gwen could do about Robert maxing out the account jointly held in their names.

Gwen was unfortunately just as liable for half of his debts as entitled to half of his earnings. Good luck with that. Robert, a successful production assistant with a Hollywood company providing East Coast sets, had found plenty of loopholes in which to stash his cash. Gwen twisted the simple wedding band once, realizing her cheeks were damp.

She finished off her chardonnay, more determined than ever to sell those canvases and at the best possible price. She'd started small with a few local juried art shows around town, then had dared to put a modest portfolio of slides together and began sending it out. Holbrook and Holstein in Santa Fe had been her first real nibble. In effect, it had been a really big bite. Top dollar for her work, plus the cost of round-trip air tickets and accommodations to boot. Holbrook probably thought that Gwen was being greedy, trying to barter up the price for her own gain. Nothing could be further from the truth. Marian's kids needed their mama, and Gwen needed to help her baby sister. One way or another, Gwen was going to see this through. Dan Holbrook could think anything about her that he liked. She'd never see him again after tomorrow anyway.

****

Chapter Two

When Dan got to La Cantina, Gwen had already arrived. He spied her seated at a table for two in the large atrium styled like a Spanish courtyard and decorated in colorful tile. She studied the menu as he approached, a white peasant blouse sweeping her shoulders, hair pinned up in a casual way that offset her cheekbones and fair complexion. Dan had to stop walking and catch his breath. She was truly a beautiful woman, even more beautiful than he'd given her credit for yesterday at the gallery. Then again, yesterday at the gallery, she'd appeared primed to bite his head off. Today, she just looked hungry.

"Can I help you find a table, sir?" a tall waiter in a waistcoat inquired.

"Thanks, I see where I'm going," Dan said, shaking the reverie. Hearing their exchange, Gwen looked up at him and smiled. He felt a little twist in his gut and realized this was worse than he thought. Dan smiled back pleasantly, determined to pull himself together. He envisioned a large Weber grill, coals searing beneath its grate, and suddenly felt driven to thirst.

He joined Gwen at the table, exchanged pleasantries, then took a long drag of water from the glass that had been provided at his place. She eyed him curiously as he drained it all.

"It's murder out there," he said, referencing the weather.

"Certainly is hot," she agreed.

"I hope you found this place okay."

"Oh yes, just fine." Warm brown eyes sparkled enticingly.

"They've got some really great specials today. Have you taken a look?"

Gwen turned over the menu in her hands, and he wondered again about that wedding band. How long had she been divorced, and why would she continue to wear it? Dan reminded himself that delving into Gwen's personal affairs was none of his business.

She surveyed the ample list of entrees. "Any recommendations?"

"Depends on whether you like spicy."

She gave him a big, appealing grin. "I love spicy food. All kinds. But I'd love to try something particular to the region." Why did she have to look so darned likable today? She really wasn't cooperating in encouraging Dan to keep his distance.

"Would you like me to order for us?" he asked, wanting to be helpful yet not wishing to overstep his bounds.

"That would be nice. Thanks." Gwen lowered her face to her menu to disguise a faint blush.

Dan fought a swell of heat, surmising there wasn't enough air in here. "Okay, be honest with me. Yes or no to avocado margaritas?"

"You weren't kidding, were you?" she asked with surprise.

"I may be many things, but I'm not really much of a kidder."

She stared at him intently, trying to read him. Dan tried to repress a smile but felt his eyes crinkle just the same.

"That was kidding, wasn't it?" she asked, waving a scolding finger.

He let loose a belly laugh, enjoying himself. "I'm afraid it was."

Gwen released a tiny puff of air, apparently relieved. "I'll try an avocado margarita," she answered, "but just one."

A little while later, Gwen took her first taste of the tantalizing southwestern treat. Finely pureed like a smoothie, it was silky, cool, and delicious. You couldn't taste the tequila at all. Gwen was glad she'd made the advance decision to stick with one. Holbrook did too. He ordered them a delicious chicken poblano over Mexican rice, with a cold gazpacho soup to start. It was a perfect meal, and he had been right. After a couple of margaritas, their conversation flowed a lot more smoothly. For one thing, she learned that while his name was on it, he didn't actually run the gallery. He was merely filling in this month for his older sister Nancy. His real work involved home building of some kind. It was a job he seemed to enjoy and which often kept him outdoors.

"I insist that you call me Dan," he said as their plates were cleared. "Mr. Holbrook hardly seems right with me calling you Gwen. You're making me feel like an old man."

"Oh, I suspect you're not that old," she said, feeling as if she was flirting.

He colored slightly around his open collar. "Thirty-nine next month. Practically over the hill."

He was dressed casually today, in khaki slacks and an azure polo shirt that complemented his eyes. The shirt fit him nicely, stretching evenly across his broad and muscled chest. Gwen found herself wondering what it would be like to press her hands against it, feel the strength and power there. Maybe that margarita was getting to her after all.

"Well, I'm thirty-two, so not that far behind you."

He took a long, slow sip of his drink, surveying her over the rim of his glass. "Something tells me it will be some time before Ms. Gwendolyn Marsh makes it over that hill."

Now was he flirting with her? The way he studied her made Gwen think Dan had more than painting on his mind. She imagined removing his shirt and applying a deep massage oil, stroking the musculature there. Heat welled within her, sending electric currents from her fingertips to her toes. Gwen reminded herself to stay on track. Maybe the margarita was getting to him as well. Although that seemed difficult to believe, given his sturdy and scrumptious build. Oh dear, there she went again. It was a relief when Dan changed the subject by suggesting dessert. Anything to take her mind off further explorations of that come-hither chest.

"It was a wonderful lunch, but I honestly don't have room for more."

"Not even jalapeño custard pie?" Dan tempted. Gwen had the sense that Dan Holbrook could tempt even the most sensible woman into almost anything.

"Maybe next time," she said, combating a new rush of heat with a long drink of water, which, instead of hitting her lips, splashed in her lap. "Oh dear!" Gwen brought her palms to her cheeks as Dan sprang from his chair.

"Take mine," he said, pressing his cloth napkin to her skirt. Suddenly, his warmth spread through her nether regions. She gasped, and he glanced up, their eyes locking.

"I'll get it, thanks," she stammered as he pulled his napkin aside, and she took to the task with hers, promptly dropping her napkin on the floor. "My goodness."

Dan scooped low to retrieve the soggy rag. He hesitated briefly to study her dangling ankle bracelet, then righted himself slowly, his sky-blue gaze grazing hers.

Dan reddened as he handed Gwen back her napkin. "I'll call the waiter over and ask for more."

"Don't bother," she said sweetly. "I think that's got it."

Gwen couldn't believe what a klutz she'd been. What was it about this man that made her all butterfingered? Okay, the truth was Marian had sometimes accused her of being a teensy bit clumsy, but she'd never been an out-and-out wrecking ball like this. It was probably a combination of things. Her mission for money complicated by Dan's inexcusable hotness. She found herself wishing briefly that his sister Nancy had been here to meet with her instead. A split-second later, she realized that was a lie.

The hard fact was Gwen was attracted to Dan. Seriously attracted. And perhaps he'd given indications that he was the slightest bit interested in her as well. But what was wrong with that? Colleagues could enjoy a simple flirtation, for heaven's sake. Gwen was sure it happened all the time. That certainly didn't mean it had to go anywhere. Gwen hadn't come to Santa Fe to find a man. She'd come to launch her art career and help her sister. Over time, she'd also be helping herself. After a while, she could do less and less of her day job and more of what gave her pleasure and caused her spirit to soar.

"You know," Dan said as coffee arrived for the two of them. "I've gone on at length about my work, and you haven't really talked about yours. Have you been painting long?"

"I did a bit in high school, but then sort of let it go."

"How's that?" he asked.

"When I started applying to colleges, my mom encouraged me to pursue something a bit more practical." She shrugged, resigned. "She may have had a point. I'm not sure what sort of job I might have gotten as an art major. I couldn't imagine teaching something I loved so much and found so personal. I'm afraid it would have taken the passion out of it for me. So I decided to finish in music instead."

"Music?" he asked with surprise. "Are you talented?"

"Not in the least," she said with a laugh. "In fact, do you know that expression?"

Dan grinned. "Those who can, do; those who can't, teach?"

"Precisely. I can't carry a tune in a bucket, and I'm impossibly inept on the keyboard."

Dan leaned forward on his elbows. "Then how…?"

"Oh, I have a great ear for things. I mean, when someone else is doing the playing, I can pluck the mistakes right out. Not that I'm hard on my students. I'm really a very encouraging teacher." And she was too. The children appeared to love her, and their parents praised her abilities. Gwen was just thankful that none of them had borne witness to her botchery of university piano recitals. It was a blessing that she could graduate in teaching without having to prove her own exceptional skill.

Dan gave a delighted chuckle. "What grades do you teach?"

"Elementary during the school year. In the summertime, I take private piano students on, all ages up to adults."

"So you could teach me?" he asked invitingly. Uh-oh, there he went, flirting again. Gwen doubted very seriously that she could teach the dangerously capable Dan Holbrook anything. At thirty-eight, he was bound to have seen a bit of the world and more than his share of women. Gwen reminded herself not to be foolishly flattered by his probably practiced attentions.

"I'm not sure about that. Something tells me you might not be the most cooperative student."

Dan raised his brows in surprise, then released another belly laugh. "You've probably got me there. Nancy tried to teach me 'Chopsticks' once when I was ten, and I never quite got through it."

Gwen couldn't help but soften at his self-effacing honesty. If she wasn't careful, she was going to start liking the man, and that might cloud her judgment in any business dealings. She finished her coffee, realizing lunch was nearly over and they'd not yet talked turkey.

"Some people have more natural talent than others," she said kindly.

"Like you do for painting, for instance," he said, turning the conversation in what Gwen hoped would be the right direction.

"I appreciate you thinking so," she said, feeling her heart warm. "I really enjoy what I do. The thought that it might also bring happiness to someone else is just wonderful."

"When did you start painting again?"

"Oh, I did it off and on. Just for me, you know. Could never entirely let it go over the years. Then on my thirtieth birthday, my little sister, Marian, gave me the most beautiful gift, a completely new set of oils and brushes. I'd been getting by with old things, mostly cast-offs from the school art teacher who'd been sympathetic to my cause."

"Marian must know you very well."

"We're super close," Gwen said, feeling the burn in her throat. "The gift was extra special because oils are expensive, and Marian... Well, she...she doesn't have a lot of money."

"So that's when it really started? When you began painting more regularly?"

Gwen nodded, willing away the unpleasant memory of Robert coming in and upending her very first seascape. *"Ridiculous,"* he'd said. *"Where do you think you'll get with that? You sure as hell can't sing. What makes you think you can paint?"*

Gwen blinked, briefly turning away. When she turned back to Dan, she found herself caught up in his sky-blue gaze. The way he looked at her was soothing, as if he had all the time in the world to listen to what she had to say, and like none of it was ridiculous.

"I did start painting more then, yes. It was easier without the resistance."

"Resistance?"

"That doesn't really matter anymore," she said, forcing a smile. "I found a way to move beyond it."

"And the clients at Holbrook and Holstein will be glad. I assure you."

"I'm glad you brought that up so I didn't have to."

He looked at her earnestly. "Gwen, I've had a great time at lunch with you, really I have. But I have no illusions about why a beautiful young woman like you would spend time with a washed-up old bachelor like me."

Gwen blushed at the compliment but wasn't about to let herself get derailed by his manly attentions. As long as he'd started the ball rolling, she needed to push it along. "You underestimate yourself, Dan. But it's good to know you've reconsidered underestimating my work."

His gaze filled with admiration. She was being a little saucy, and he apparently liked it. "I spoke with Nancy like I promised. Holbrook and Holstein is prepared to set a fair price for your art. We can't quite go up to four thousand, but if you're willing to agree to three-five, we think we can cut a deal."

The way he'd said that made it almost seem real, as if this was actually going to happen for her. Gwen tried to contain her excitement. "Excellent," she said, giving him what she hoped was a warm, even smile. "I'm open to discussing that."

"Of course, I'm sure you're familiar with how things work," he continued. "Gallery sales are commission based, so whatever price we arrive at is provisional."

The corners of Gwen's mouth took a downturn. The fact was, she didn't know this at all. "I'm sorry. I'm not sure what you're saying."

Dan set his empty coffee cup aside and laced his fingers together in a sincere fashion. "I'm saying the gallery takes a commission. That's how it stays in business. Your work for sale there is basically on consignment."

The shock and horror hit her in the stomach like a sucker punch. "Consignment? But nothing in Ms. Holstein's email said anything about—"

His gaze softened, genuinely apologetic. "I'm sorry, Gwen. She probably thought you knew. Most of the artists we deal with are…experienced."

Gwen felt a flash of anger, but she quelled it, realizing nobody had intentionally tried to mislead her. "Are you saying I won't be getting any money now?" she asked, trying to mask the desperation in her voice.

"Now?" he asked, as if he'd never considered the possibility. "You mean, like during your ten-day trip to Santa Fe?

"Gwen, we're dealing with a process, here. We agree on what we think a reasonable buyer might pay in this market. That is the sale price. The two of us sign a contract, and then you ship the canvases. Once they're here, we hang them up for sale. As money comes in, it's funneled directly to you, less the gallery's twenty-percent commission."

Gwen felt her entire world crumbling in on her. Maybe it was her fault, hoping for too much in just one visit. But what if things didn't sell? What if enough money didn't come on time? What if the bank failed to extend its credit?

Gwen thought of Marian and her kids, of lives pulling apart... Of Robert's repeated infidelities... Her art box being tossed into the ocean... Something cut loose inside, and she felt like she might lose it at any second, break down sobbing on this already soppy napkin. She opened her purse and pulled out a tissue.

Dan reached a steadying hand across the table and laid it on hers. "Gwen? Are you all right?"

"Excuse me," she said, dabbing the corner of her eye. "I'll be right back."

Dan sat there for the longest time, wondering what he'd done wrong. Could Gwen truly have thought she'd fly out of here in just over a week with wads of cash lining her pockets? Were her circumstances really that bad? She'd seemed so fragile when she'd rushed out of here, as if she might break apart at any minute. Dan had no idea what sort of situation she was in, but he did know one thing. If he could, he wanted to help.

After what seemed like an eternity, Gwen resurfaced, all fresh-faced with newly applied lipstick and powder. Dan was finally starting to understand why women kept so much nonsense in their purses. It was for emergency situations like this.

"Any better?" he asked with concern.

She gave a sniff and lifted her chin.

"Allergies. Never know when they're going to hit me."

"Glad you're okay."

"Yes," she said, taking her seat. "Just fine, thanks." She noted the credit card receipt on the table. "Oh, you've already paid the bill. I'm sorry. I didn't mean for you to—"

"My pleasure," he said, meaning it. He hadn't had a lunch this interesting with a woman in a decade. Everything he'd learned about Gwen had been fascinating. But what intrigued him most was all that he didn't know. "Gwen," he began, hoping to broach the subject lightly. "I couldn't help but notice you were a little…thrown by our arrangement."

"The consignment, you mean?" she asked proudly. "Oh no, I knew all about it. I suspected that's how things went." It was a brave cover, but Dan saw straight through it. Didn't help her that her chin still trembled slightly.

"That's how it normally goes," he answered. "But there's really no need for us to go getting all bogged down in normalcy, wouldn't you say?"

She knitted her delicately sculpted brow. "I'm sorry? I'm not sure I follow."

A few gold tendrils broke free from their pins and spilled forward. Dan had an idiotic impulse to reach out and sweep them back, chancing a touch of her alabaster skin. He stopped himself just in time, tucking away the bill receipt in his pocket instead. "How soon can you get your canvases out here?"

"To Santa Fe? Why, in just a few days. They're all packaged and ready to ship."

"That settles it, then," he said with a wide, easy grin.

"Settles what? I haven't signed any contract."

"No, but if you will, I have an idea," he said slyly.

"What sort of idea is that?" she whispered, angling forward.

Dan looked straight in her eyes with calm reassurance. "We don't normally operate this fast, but I do have a list of potential buyers I can contact."

Her face lit up like the most stunning sunrise. "Are you saying what I think you are?"

"If fortune smiles on us, we might be able to sell a canvas or two before you leave."

"All five?" she asked with a hopeful glow.

Dan feared he'd done the wrong thing, caused her to think it was a certainty that this would go off. But when she'd gone all weepy on him, it had been impossible for Dan to stop himself. The truth was he had the means to buy all five of Gwen's canvases himself without even making a dent in his money-market account. But that would make the dealings between them personal, and Dan had vowed to keep things on a professional level.

Dan returned her gaze with cautious determination. "Let's not go pushing our luck," he said, sensing he'd gotten in over his head. He envisioned a huge, raw T-bone getting tossed onto a grill. Perspiration built at his brow, and he lifted Gwen's soggy napkin from the table to dab it.

"I need to get back to work," he said, standing and helping Gwen with her chair. "Think you might stop by later to sign the papers? The gallery closes at eight. That would be a good time."

"Eight o'clock it is," she said with a smile that knocked his socks off and held potential to knock other items of clothing off too.

Dan said a polite good-bye, then hustled out of there like a rabbit being hunted by a pack of wild coyotes. He needed to get his head together and figure his way through these next few days. Not that this should be a problem for a take-charge guy like him who knew how and where to draw the line.

Dan knew it was for the best, and really in Gwen's interest, for him to back off from any sort of romantic notions now, while the backing was good. No matter what

Santa Fean magazine said about Dan being the "Best Billionaire Bachelor Catch in the West," privately he knew his shortcomings would give even the most understanding woman pause. Dan had been down that dusty trail once and was determined never to go there again. Didn't matter what sort of attractive filly came out of the gate. The fact of the matter was Dan wasn't riding.

****

Chapter Three

Gwen left the restaurant by exiting onto the main plaza, an oasis of green in the earth-toned adobe town. Huge shade trees lined its crisscrossing sidewalks, dotted with wrought-iron benches and lampposts. Bordered by the nation's oldest public building, the Palace of Governors, on one side and an array of upscale shops on the others, it was the city's central gathering spot and playground, complete with a bandstand in which an impromptu flautist played. Gwen strode past a snow-cone vendor and a couple of quesadilla carts on her way to explore the smattering of handmade goods the locals had spread on the ground atop woven blankets. She surveyed the assorted silver jewelry, accented with turquoise, and small trinkets for sale with an appreciative eye, and made complimentary small talk with the Native American and Mexican peoples proudly showcasing their wares.

A warm breeze blew as the sun angled high, bathing Santa Fe in its rosy glow, the impressive Sangre de Cristo Mountains just visible in the distance, their highest peaks capped with snow, even in summertime. Gwen made her way up a side street to visit Saint Francis Cathedral, a stunning Romanesque Revival structure challenging the surrounding adobe architecture with its sweeping arches and brightly hued stained-glass windows.

Perspiration dampened her hairline as she climbed the steps to the building's entrance. It was warmer in the sunlight, the scarcely filtered ultraviolet rays bearing down on her, causing her feet and hands to swell. At once, the thin gold band on her left ring finger felt too tight. She twisted it slightly as she continued her ascent toward the cathedral's front door. Gwen hadn't prayed for anything in a long time. In fact, she hadn't been to church since Robert left. Maybe she should have. Thinking it over, she understood she had much to be thankful for. Not least among her blessings was her opportunity to come here.

Gwen passed through the enormous wooden door, her senses immediately engulfed by burning incense. Though she wasn't Catholic, she didn't believe God would mind if she took a spot on a pew for a few moments to mull through her life. What an event it had been. There'd been so much to it she'd never seen coming. When she met Robert in college, he'd appeared so promising. He was ambitious and fun and seemed poised to carve out a good life for himself and any lady lucky enough to join him. When he'd asked Gwen to marry him just before graduation, she'd been over the moon. He had a good job offer in Wilmington, and they could settle in the nearby town where Gwen had grown up and her family still lived. It had all seemed so idyllic at first.

Gwen glanced down at the completely ineffectual wedding ring as her hand rested in her lap. It hadn't taken long for Robert to find someone he thought more intelligent and interesting than her. She bored him to tears with her tales of kids in school and had no real talents as far as he could gather. The people he worked with were insightful, intuitive, interesting… Maybe if Gwen looked more at the papers or followed the news, she'd be interesting too, though he kind of doubted it.

Gwen heaved a sigh, knowing she couldn't continue to beat herself up over Robert's shortcomings. When she was thinking clearly, as Marian often encouraged her to do, she understood that her marriage falling apart had more to do with him than her. Or perhaps it was due to them both and the fact that, once they'd escaped from the cocoonlike sanctuary of the university, neither of them truly fit together. Gwen wondered sadly if she was destined to fit together with any man. Perhaps that wasn't in the cards for her, and maybe that was okay. If her art took off and she built herself a career, something that she adored and was really proud of, that might be enough.

She considered her meeting this evening with Dan, realizing she'd been acting like a silly schoolgirl. It wasn't his fault she hadn't dated since her divorce, so why should she hold him accountable for her surging hormones? Any nice-looking man who'd paid her attention would likely have made her feel the same. As an elementary schoolteacher, she simply hadn't had much opportunity for that. All the men she met were either married or formerly married and quickly reattached. It seemed the decent ones didn't last long on the market. From what she'd gathered from her quick perusals of Internet dating sites, the perpetual bachelors all seemed to have something wrong with them. Then again, Dan appeared normal. Exceedingly normal, healthy, and sexually enticing as well. So why hadn't a tamale-hot catch like him been snapped up already?

Gwen decided to head back to the inn to cool off for a few hours before her gallery appointment. This praying business didn't seem to be going too well. She thought she'd probably done it wrong. It had been such a while, she couldn't tell. In any case, she was grateful to Dan for granting her this chance. At the heart of it, Gwen understood that was all this really was, a chance to sell some of her art to a very fine place and hopefully help turn her sister's life around. That was worth a few amens, no doubt. She dipped her head, offering them quickly, and bowed out of the cathedral before anyone could stop her and ask her for money. That was one part of going to church she hadn't forgotten. There was a lady near the door collecting donations for the restoration fund. Gwen slipped silently past her and out into the sunshine before the woman could hold up a brochure. Maybe once Gwen was rich and famous she'd feel a bit more philanthropic. At the moment, she scarcely had cash for dinner. She'd have to hurry to catch the wine-and-cheese hour before the other guests cleaned out the Havarti.

Dan paced the redwood-pine floors, double-checking the time on his BlackBerry. The afternoon couldn't have dragged out more if he'd planned it. It all seemed to go in slow motion, as if he were deep-sea diving, arms and legs battling against ocean pressure.

The occasional browsers stopped by, and there was the shipment to get out to Los Angeles, but Nancy's assistant Megan had come in to see to that. She wore a nose piercing and a puckish haircut that added to her image of a small sprite sprinting around the gallery. Dan had never seen a twenty-three-year-old with so much energy. She was very astute though, her nimble mind eager to acquire anything and everything about gallery running. She hoped to manage a place of her own one day and apparently did some sort of printmaking on the side.

"That's it, then," Megan said, peering up at him through heavily mascaraed eyes. "Think that I might sneak out early? I've got a date for drinks at Nines." Nines was the hipster bar on an adobe rooftop overlooking the mountains.

"Don't let me hold you back," Dan said.

"Are you all right?" Megan asked. "You've seemed a little…off this afternoon. Maybe you should head out early too."

Dan was more than a little off; he was distractingly discombobulated. He'd spent over three hours poring through Nancy's customary client list, trying to discern those who might be interested in Gwen's work. If he'd had his head on straight, the task might have taken him forty-five minutes. Instead, he'd caught himself daydreaming at every turn, reliving his lively lunch with Ms. Gwendolyn Marsh. Just as in the gallery the day before, he'd been sucked in by the feminine scent of her. Didn't help one iota that she obviously perfumed her legs, legs that were attached to one knock-out of a womanly body, teamed with a damnably adorable and kissable, he couldn't help but reason, face. And, when her eyes sparked with delight at the thought that he might help her, could actually sell her canvases in this absurd ten-day timeframe, Dan's heart had done an unexpected flip-flop.

"I'm fine," he lied to Megan. "Why don't you go on ahead? I've got an artist stopping by at closing. I'll lock up."

Megan grabbed her colorful straw bag that looked large enough to hold a weekend wardrobe and pranced out the door.

Dan strode to the desk and withdrew Gwen's contract from the nearby filing cabinet. He glanced through the folder for maybe the tenth time today, ensuring everything was in order. The paperwork was all lined up. Now all Dan had to do was steel his heart. He was getting far too carried away with this. Just because Gwen looked like an angel and spoke in a sweet Southern twang that was sexy as sin, that didn't mean he'd have to give in to her. He was a rational man, by all accounts, savvy at business dealings and skilled at keeping his emotions in check.

Okay, he'd made that one mistake. But it wasn't like it was going to come back to haunt him. It had been more than a month now, and he'd heard nothing further about it. It had been a harsh lesson in letting sleeping dogs lie. Once you make a pact to move on, there should be no looking back. Looking ahead wasn't sounding so safe at the moment either. Gwen was scheduled to be in town only ten days. She had her life back East to lead, and Dan had his own ghosts to contend with here. He shook off a gloomy feel, determined to make the best of their meeting. Dan was sensible enough to know he could assist a damsel in distress without falling into bed with her. And just to make certain he hadn't forgotten, the fates had pressed a branding iron to his chest a mere six weeks ago to drive that message home.

Gwen tugged at the zipper of her skirt, sliding it up her ample hip. She'd put on a few pounds since her divorce but still looked okay, she supposed. She'd never been accused of being overly thin. Marian was the slight one in the family, while Gwen fought the perpetual battle of the booty. Breasts, hips, and thighs had a will of their own. No matter how she tried, they relished maintaining their prefab form. After a while, Gwen had just given up and decided to enjoy life. As long as she operated within reason, didn't diet or exercise too much, she could stay within the same five-pound range that she'd grown accustomed to and certain men seemed to appreciate.

Gwen flushed at the memory of Dan's sky-blue gaze. At first she'd thought he'd just been flattering her, trying to put a gallery contact at ease. But the more she pondered it, the less she thought so. As they'd sat there discussing canvas pricing, his heated perusal had washed all over her like the clearest Caribbean wave. Gwen imagined the two of them on a distant beach, Dan bare-chested in the sun. He'd tell her once more how beautiful she was, and, half-naked in her tummy-control swimsuit, she'd feel forced to believe it. He'd take her by the waist then, pull her soft body to his, taut stomach muscles tensing as he wrapped his arms around her... Gwen heard the surf crash, water swirling furiously at their feet, as he brought his glorious mouth to hers.

Suddenly, she realized she'd stalled in applying her lipstick and was standing there all puckered up like a ridiculous guppy. "That's the price I pay for that second Shiraz," she scolded herself, vowing to make coffee. She was glad the suite's miniature kitchen supplied what she needed for that. Now where was the sugar cube she could find to quell her outlandish fantasies?

Gwen had considered putting on a flirty dress for her meeting with Dan tonight but now worried that might send the wrong message. She wasn't seeing him for any sort of social reasons, she reminded herself. They were convening to sign a contract, for heaven's sake. Gwen lifted her perfume bottle and spritzed her neck, wrists, and the backs of her knees with its fine aroma.

Gwen's belly warmed as she recalled how Dan had hesitated by her foot just an instant too long in retrieving her dropped napkin. If he'd touched her then, even by accidentally brushing her calf, she would have fainted. They would have had to call in the rescue squad to scoop her limp form off the New Mexican tile. It didn't take an expert to see the super-studly Dan Holbrook held more masculinity in one pinkie than the pallid and self-possessed Robert contained from head to toe.

Coffee, Gwen reminded herself, noting by the clock on the nightstand it was almost time. The sooner she got this over and done with, the better. If she could negotiate the paperwork without chancing to shake Dan's hand, all the better. Even after the coffee, Gwen didn't trust herself to touch him. This was what Marian called an unwelcome consequence of celibacy.

Gwen adjusted her bra, shifting her bosom into its proper place, then, quite as an afterthought, she was sure, gave her cleavage the tiniest little burst of Midnight Jasmine perfume.

Dan looked up as the door chime sounded. There she stood, looking as gorgeous as a desert sunset, the colors of her sexy, short dress swirling about her in mauve, gold, and russet browns. "Are you ready for me?" she asked, dark eyes sparkling with anticipation.

Dan thought he was, in fact had prepared for her all afternoon, but now he felt as awkward and uncertain as a teenager. "Of course," he said, working to get the words out in a businesslike manner. "Come on in." Her womanly scent overtook him as his eyes trailed from her ankles to her cleavage to her faintly colored cheekbones. "Please, have a seat." He indicated a spot, nearly missing his own chair. Dan scooted onto it as she pulled hers in toward the desk just a tad too close. The sweet angles of her knees pressed into his ever so slightly.

A crimson blush warmed her shoulders and swept up her delicate throat. "Oh! Oh my goodness. I'm so sorry!" she cried, backing up.

"No worries! Really," he protested.

Gwen sat up a little straighter in her chair and crossed her legs as Dan opened the file in front of him. He passed her the paperwork with an appreciative gaze.

"You look lovely tonight," he said, unable to stop himself.

Gwen met his eyes, her cheeks still aglow. "Thank you. You look…really super too."

Dan reined himself in, applying his best businesslike tone. "I believe everything's in order there," he said as she fanned through the pages. "If you'd like to look it over, I can answer any questions."

The sun dipped low outside, casting a tangerine hue throughout the wide-open spaces of the gallery as Gwen sorted through the agreement. After a few moments of studied concentration, she addressed Dan with a relieved smile. "It all seems straightforward." She'd worried it might be complicated, filled with legalese and fine-print sections. On the contrary, it basically laid out what they had discussed at lunch, with a few boilerplate clauses she supposed were included in most contracts of this kind. "Where do I sign?"

Dan indicated the line, then added his own signature to the page.

"Have you come up with any contacts? I mean, people who might buy my art?"

Dan smiled indulgently. "Don't you think we ought to get it here first?"

"Right! I'll have Marian send it out tomorrow. Like I said, it's all boxed and ready to go. All she has to do is call for shipping."

Dan wrote some numbers on a small notepad on the desk. "This is our account number for Southwest Express. Have your sister call this phone number and bill it to us. She can let them know where and when to pick up the packages."

"Well, thanks, that's very gracious. That will help a lot." Gwen couldn't let him know that her wallet was paper-thin or that her sister was destitute.

"I've actually already sent out a couple of emails, feelers, if you will, to gallery contacts who might have an interest in an East Coast ocean scene or two."

Gwen felt her face warm with excitement. "That's wonderful!" She fought an urge to race around the desk and hug him.

"As soon as the pieces arrive," he continued, "I'll start making follow-up calls. I'm hoping to have some serious buyers in looking by the end of the week. Assuming the shipment goes as planned."

Gwen sprang from her seat and lunged for his hand. "I don't know how to thank you," she said, taking his hand in hers and holding it firmly.

His gaze wrapped around her, trapping her in his heat. "It's my pleasure, really," he said, exerting delicate pressure against her palm. Little tingles raced up Gwen's arm, and instantly she knew she'd made a mistake. She'd told herself to keep her distance. Now, all she wanted to do was get closer still. Gwen released his grip, attempting to steady herself on wobbly knees. If merely shaking hands had this much effect, she'd hate to see the pool of putty she'd be in if he'd dared to kiss her.

"Have you eaten anything since lunch?" he asked with concern.

Gwen pulled herself together, realizing she must have suddenly paled. "I had some wine and cheese back at the inn."

"Havarti?" he asked, with uncanny insight.

"How did you…?"

He repressed a grin, pointing to the back of her head. Gwen ran panicked fingers through her hair, finding a nice little chunk of cheese caught up in her curls.

She stared at him, mortified. "I'm so embarrassed," she began.

"Don't be," he offered kindly. "I get Camembert in mine all the time."

She scanned his face for the hint of a smile but couldn't detect one beneath his deadpan.

"This time, I know you're teasing," she said, and the moment between them lightened.

Small lines tugged at the corners of his mouth as blue eyes crinkled. "Something tells me you're getting to know me too well." His gaze held a hint of longing mixed with caution. "Wine and cheese isn't much of a dinner. I know a place with great steaks, if you'd like to join me?"

Gwen knew she was wrong to say yes. Everything inside her screamed *caution, slippery roads ahead*. But all Gwen wanted to do was get in that spectacular sports car and drive.

"I'd love to," she said, accepting his invitation.

Dan led them down a side street to an elegant outdoor restaurant set a few blocks from the plaza. The shaded pathway to its entrance bypassed the abutting Loretto Chapel, a notable nineteenth-century structure in Gothic Revival style, complete with buttresses and spires.

"Have you been in there?" Dan asked as they strolled by the wind art adorning the chapel's lawn.

Gwen admired the huge hands of the whimsical brass structures cupping and turning in the breeze as the sun sank low. "Not yet."

Her view panned to a fanciful wood carving of a man guarding the chapel door.

"Saint Joseph," Dan said, indicating the statue. "I'll tell you the story over dinner. You do believe in miracles?" He was smiling at her in a playful way.

A shiver shimmied down Gwen's spine, as she thought it was nothing short of miraculous that she was here, right now, with him. Dan Holbrook was not just a feast for the eyes, he was funny and kind and apparently enjoying her company. Plus, he made her feel beautiful. Not just because he'd said it. It was in the way he looked at her, all the time.

"I'll keep an open mind," she said, smiling back at him.

Dan shoved his hand in his pocket to prevent himself from reaching out and taking hers. In some ways, it would have seemed natural as he led her toward the maître d. In others, it was completely absurd! Dan heaved a sigh, grateful good sense had prevailed.

"Are you all right?" she asked, chocolate-brown eyes imploring.

"Just taking in the evening," he said, thankful there was no wait for a table.

He ordered them filet mignon with a mushroom, red pepper, and sherry reduction, Caesar salads to start, and a choice bottle of Chilean red wine. Dan didn't want to mess this up. Gwen's dinner had to be perfect. He'd slipped the maître d an unseen tip to ensure it. He'd also told Gwen upfront that the meal was on him. He'd seen the way her brow had knitted slightly as she'd surveyed the menu prices. Dan wasn't sure what sort of money trouble she was in, but he could bet her budget didn't include places like this one.

"The service is fabulous here," Gwen said as her water glass magically refilled.

Dan had the impression Gwen wasn't used to men treating her right. He was glad to be able to change that, to show her that not all men were schmucks, maybe just the ones she'd previously run into. "Wait until you taste the food."

She smiled sweetly over the rim of her wineglass. "This carménère is delicious. I'm so glad I got to try it."

"Should go well with the steak," Dan said, hoping he'd scored a point. For the life of him, he wanted to impress this woman. She looked prettier than ever, sitting there relaxed in the candle's glow. He compared her now to how she'd appeared yesterday afternoon in the gallery, anxiously combative, like if he didn't see things her way, there'd be hell to pay. He probably liked this Gwen better. Though the truth of the matter was Dan didn't really mind the other one much at all. He could see a man getting used to a balanced measure of them both.

Dan took a sip of wine, knowing he was letting his emotions get the best of him. That was a dangerous mountain to climb when he understood what was on the other side: a clean downhill slide where his heart would take a tumble. Elena had been quite detailed in enumerating his faults.

A crescent moon rose as a smattering of stars poured onto the canvas of the night sky above them. Their salads arrived, artfully served and in a timely fashion.

"So, are you going to tell me the story?" she asked eagerly.

Dan was happy for the chance to take his mind off his gloomy thoughts. "Ah yes, the story of Loretto Chapel," he said, setting down his glass. He leaned forward on his elbows and lowered his voice. "And its mysterious spiral staircase."

"Staircase?" she asked with surprise.

"Legend has it the staircase in Loretto Chapel arrived as a miracle. Some to this day may dispute it, but many others do not."

"Go on," she pressed, intrigued.

"Rumor holds that when the chapel was completed in the eighteen hundreds, the dear nuns who lived there noted there was no staircase to get them to the choir loft on the upper level."

"Oh my!"

"So they prayed for nine days for a miracle. On the tenth day, an unknown carpenter appeared and offered to complete the task. He built the freestanding staircase all by himself without using glue, nails, or any central support. Then, as soon as he was done, the stranger disappeared just as mysteriously as he'd arrived, without ever having identified himself or demanding any payment. The good sisters of Loretto naturally took this as a miracle, and the man to have been Saint Joseph himself. The proof I believe lies in the number of steps of the freestanding structure, made of a wood not even found in this region."

"Well?" she asked, her eyes twinkling.

"Thirty-three. The age of Jesus Christ."

Gwen leaned back in her chair with a delighted laugh. "That's wonderful! What a fantastic story."

"It's not a story," he said with mock defensiveness. "It's a miracle." The corners of his mouth twitched slightly, and Gwen could tell he was repressing a smile. She was finally starting to read him, and for a girl who didn't like to read, that said a lot.

Gwen cocked an eyebrow and shot him an impish smile. "Do you believe in miracles, Dan?"

He captured her with his gaze, stilling her heart for a fraction of a second. "Let's just say I believe most things in life can be rationally explained."

"Most things don't mean all," she bantered lightly.

He raised his glass to hers as their salad plates were cleared and the entrées arrived. "You've got me there."

Everything smelled delicious. Gwen couldn't wait to dig in. She hadn't realized how hungry she'd gotten subsisting on complimentary inn food these past few days.

"How's your filet?" he asked as she took a heavenly bite that literally melted in her mouth. "Cooked all right?"

He was incredibly handsome in the soft light, flames from the outdoor fire caressing the solid lines of his face.

"Perfect. Everything's just perfect. I couldn't have had a better night."

"I'm glad," he said with a grin. "That just leaves tomorrow."

"What do you mean?"

"You've got a bit of time to kill while the shipment comes in. Got any plans?"

"I thought I'd take in an art museum or two."

"That sounds great. I've been considering taking the day off myself."

Gwen set down her fork. "Are you…asking me on a date?"

"You mean unlike this one," he deadpanned.

She gasped with surprise. "This was a date?"

"It could be if you wanted it to."

Gwen's heart went fluttering in all sorts of wild directions. Why on earth was he doing this? Surely there was no sense in it. She'd be gone by the week's end. "I'm not so sure that's a good idea."

"Which one?"

"This a date… Tomorrow. I…I don't know." And she didn't, she really didn't. She was feeling all jumbled up inside, like she'd desperately wanted something and now didn't know what to do once she'd gotten it.

"How about if we just call it an appointment, then? An arrangement between associates to go and see some art.

Besides," he added temptingly, "I know who serves the best chile rellenos in town."

It was patently unfair of him to play the food card. Gwen absolutely adored chile rellenos, almost as much as she was starting to adore this man. "It's a deal," she said, smiling broadly.

Dan walked Gwen back to the inn, night sounds singing around them. He'd really jumped in headlong with this one, but Dan couldn't completely blame himself. With her lovely looks and warm and charming personality, Gwen had led him right to it. He'd been having such a good time with her at dinner, he couldn't bear having the evening end. The only remedy for that was to suggest seeing her tomorrow. He didn't have much going on at the gallery, and what was left to do Megan could take care of.

Dan stole a glimpse of Gwen strolling beside him in the moonlight and wished for a moment that things weren't transitory. But they were, and he'd need to remain aware of that. Just because they'd planned to spend the day together didn't mean they'd have to become any more involved than they already were. He liked Gwen, dammit. She was sensitive and sweet, and he felt good when he was around her. Dan hadn't felt this good about himself in a very long while. He decided it was time.

They got to the exterior patio door of Gwen's private suite, and she opened her purse to withdraw the key, her cheeks still aflame.

"I had a really great time tonight," she said, beaming up at him and feeling very much as if it had been a date.

"Me too," he said, stepping a fraction of an inch closer. Sea-blue eyes washed over her, threatening to pull her under. And boy, did she want to get swept away. "I'm glad you agreed to see me tomorrow, even if it's just an arrangement."

Gwen sensed Dan could rearrange her heart every which way, if she wasn't careful. "I'm glad I'm seeing you too," she said, feeling the warmth in her cheeks.

"Ten o'clock work for you?" he asked, his tone growing gravelly.

"Uh-huh," she uttered, mesmerized by his gaze.

He moved nearer now, his mouth just inches away. "I'll be damned if I don't want to kiss you," he said, his voice a husky rasp.

And she'd be damned if she didn't want him to. "Dan…" she said, tilting up her chin and closing her eyes.

"But I won't," he said, snapping her back to attention, eyes open. "Not now. Not here. Not like this…"

She started to speak as he brought his fingers to her lips. "If ever I've seen a woman who deserves to be kissed well, it's you. But the timing has got to be right. You have to be sure." He cast a cursory glance at her wedding band and backed away. "I need to be sure. Something tells me we've both gone down a path neither of us wants to travel again."

Gwen's heart sank as her face burned hot. He was right, and she knew it. Neither of them could risk foolishly giving themselves away. It was only a kiss, but a kiss was often the beginning. She was old enough to know that, and Dan clearly was too.

Gwen couldn't guess who'd broken Dan's heart, but he'd obviously been hurt just as much as she had.

"Good night, Gwen," he said, shadows haunting his face.

She watched him turn and walk away, loneliness settling inside her like a large, heavy weight Gwen feared she'd never shake.

She let herself into her empty room and cried softly in the darkness, moonlight weeping in through slanted blinds. If only she'd found a man like Dan ten years ago, maybe neither of them would have had to live through these vestiges of pain. But the past was long ago and should be forgotten, Gwen thought, twisting the ring on her finger.

Perhaps meeting Dan now was a good thing, the right thing for them both. Maybe they were meant to be stepping stones, each of them strategically placed to help the other on to a better life. They could be friends, confidants even, during her short stay in Santa Fe. Maybe they'd each give the other someone to lean on, somebody who really understood, for the first time in a long time. That didn't mean they'd have to start falling in love.

Gwen sucked in a breath, praying it wasn't already too late. By the way her heart hammered against her chest, she wasn't sure.

****

End of excerpt from *Santa Fe Fortune*

Ginny Baird thanks you for reading her work and hopes to hear from you soon.